LIVING THINGS

MUNIR HACHEMI

TRANSLATED BY JULIA SANCHES

COACH HOUSE BOOKS, TORONTO

Cosas vivas © Munir Hachemi, 2018

The English edition is published by arrangement with Editorial Periférica c/o MB Agencia Literaria S.L.

Translation copyright © Julia Sanches, 2024

Originally published by Fitzcarraldo Editions in Great Britain in 2024

LIBRARY AND ARCHIVES CANADA CATALOGUING IN PUBLICATION

Title: Living things / Munir Hachemi ; translated by Julia Sanches.

Other titles: Cosas vivas. English

Names: Hachemi, Munir, author. | Sanches, Julia, translator.

Description: Translation of: Cosas vivas.

Identifiers: Canadiana (print) 20240289609 | Canadiana (ebook) 20240289633 | ISBN 9781552454770 (softcover) | ISBN 9781770568044 (PDF) | ISBN 9781770568037 (EPUB)

Subjects: LCGFT: Novels.

Classification: LCC PQ6708.A34 C613 2024 | DDC 863/.7—dc23

Living Things is available as an ebook: ISBN 978 1 77056 803 7 (EPUB), ISBN 978 1 77056 804 4 (PDF)

Purchase of the print version of this book entitles you to a free digital copy. To claim your ebook of this title, please email sales@chbooks.com with proof of purchase. (Coach House Books reserves the right to terminate the free digital download offer at any time.)

To the four protagonists of this story.

TABLE OF CONTENTS

1.
ARTIFICIAL RESPIRATION

We can't change reality,
but we can change the subject.
– James Joyce, as cited by Ricardo Piglia

The day I met my friend G, he told me that as a kid he devised a theory about short stories that stayed with him all his life. It shouldn't come as a surprise that the purpose of stories is to classify, to impose order and hierarchy on the real world. But reality is a wilderness – a jungle or desert – a place that cannot be mapped. Every time something wild disrupted his life, my friend G would tell a story, any story, it didn't matter what, anything would do. His parents would be screaming at each other at home, and he'd start talking about how the girl he liked had tripped in class, or how the baker had short-changed him, or whatever. He kept up this habit, or tic, as he got older – or maybe the truth is that he never lost it – and went on perfecting his theory. 'Listen, the cut-off point between the way we cast light on the world and the world itself is the exact moment when that light is lost: death. Every civilization has built its identity – its cosmology or *Weltan-schauung* – around this point. I can't think of a single work of fiction where someone dies without saying or at least trying to say last words, words that are then subjected to interpretative violence, as if they were a summary or sublimation of everything that person had thought, felt, and believed throughout the course of their life.' I agreed with him because he was right, or at least I thought he was, and also because I always agreed with him. As the years passed, G took this argument to the extreme and said something that could have gone on to become his last words. Roughly, that 'stories were born the moment our ancestors experienced great terror, the moment before one of them died, or when their camp was under siege, or when they lost a loved one.' That probably wasn't what he said word for word; his exact phrasing no doubt did a better job of enshrining his thanatotic theory about short fiction. For him stories were intimately connected to death, and one could not be grasped without the other. With time, this theory impacted his relationship with the world, and he began to see proof that he was right all around him. Of course, the same applies to all theories, but among G's various talents is an ability to drum up the most ingenious proofs, examples that linger in the minds of his listeners. I clearly remember him referring more than once to the scene in *Pulp Fiction* where Samuel L. Jackson has a gun pointed at him and starts talking about an epiphany he had, something his interlocutor finds incomprehensible and yet in that moment makes perfect sense to that character (and to the viewer). Stories as a way of momentarily forgetting death, stepping into death, or simply looking the other way as life carries on.

G would say that the story I'm about to tell is less a story than it is a prayer to ward off the horror that has been whispering to me for years. Maybe he's right. But I'm going to tell my story – or our story – anyway, and even more rightfully, by hewing to the truth. So don't expect to find any embellishments here beyond the ones imposed by language – which I realize are more than a few. A pessimist would insist that language inflicts so many nuances and misunderstandings – which, by the way, are not the collateral damage of language but the conditions of its existence – that the difference between the most straightforward writers and the most prolix, between the most sincere and the ones who take great pains to cut rubies out of lies, that this difference, I say – or rather, a pessimist *would say* – accounts for less than three or four per cent of all textual embellishment. I'm inclined to take a more positive approach, one less faithful or perhaps more straightforward, and start counting the flourishes at the point where language allows us to speak for ourselves: what you might call *embellishment degree zero*.

There are dozens of authors who have engaged in a cheap literary tradition that seems to take a variety of forms, all of them extremely poor. I'm talking about found manuscripts, false testimonies, and *mises en abyme*. More than a few writers have dabbled in these sorts of gimmicks, convinced they were inventing literature anew when all they were doing was proving how little they cared about it. Paradoxically, I – who do not consider myself a writer (not any more) – will be the first to declare that the emperor has no clothes, the first to take the floor with the courage needed to flout the frills and artifice, the first to tell the story as it unfolded and nothing more. Time will banish the rest of them to the depths of history. For now, my act of revenge will be to withhold their names.

Before I begin my story, I should give a couple of examples of the kind of literature I want to avoid. In the pages after this preface, you may come across a sentence like 'everything is covered in blood.' If that happens, don't try to tease out any hidden meaning. I'm not saying that horror coats everything like a fine, invisible film; nor does the image signify sexual desire or the urge to kill. All you should understand is that everything is covered in blood. The snow, the gravel, the houses, the lamp posts. Everything. And not fresh blood either, but dry blood – extremely dry. Another example: if I describe a scene where a person is wearing a baseball cap, don't try to tease out a metaphor. There is no metaphor. Just picture someone in a baseball cap. Whatever hermeneutic violence you unleash on this image should be no greater than the violence you unleash on the real world. In other words, this text is only a book inasmuch as everything is a book. That's it. There is no intent, just storytelling.

Embellishment degree zero. If you do your best to read it this way, then I should be able to tell you my story –the real story, what actually happened.

11.

MEMORIES OF UNDERDEVELOPMENT

The car was parked on the street where three out of the four of us lived. The trunk was open, and we were loading in our luggage while waiting for G. His being late surprised us less than the amount of stuff he had with him. He'd brought a flamenco guitar, a backpack full of books, and a load of random equipment that, if I'm remembering correctly, he'd found at his grandfather's farm. We all laughed at the beekeeping gloves, the coveralls, the ridiculously high boots. That day – this much is true – everything made us laugh. For example, we cracked up when we noticed we had each packed at least one instrument. Keep in mind that Ernesto was a pretty serious guy, Alejandro wished he was, and G – probably the smartest of us four – lived and breathed militant Marxism the way some people do literature, that is, like a rare sin of youth, a categorical decision he didn't remember making. It's possible he kept analyzing things while we laughed. It's possible he laughed with us while also thinking about how it wasn't really a coincidence, that at the end of the day the four musicians in question were four middle-class guys (lower-middle, in his case; middle-middle in mine and Álex's; upper-middle in Ernesto's – in any event, back then everyone in Spain belonged to some variation of the middle class unless proven otherwise), that three of us had read the same subject at university – you'll have guessed which of us by now – and, in short, that sociology had already concluded our similarities would far outweigh our differences. To the series of points G could have made, I'd add one that I knew about at the time but didn't have the courage to voice: not one of us was travelling for financial gain.

It's a well-known fact that all modern fiction is born out of market tension. Becoming an author entails acquiring money and fame, yet the line between the moment a person becomes an author and the moment, in so doing, they cease to be one is tenuous. Equally well-known is the theory that below the surface of every story lies another, purportedly deeper tale. This text – which is not a short story – does not have to fit this theory, while our life – a story we constantly tell ourselves – does. In a short piece by Hemingway – an author I otherwise despise – there is a couple arguing in a hotel room. The woman sees a cat on the street, I can't remember whether before – while they were taking a walk or having a drink – or in that moment – through the window. The second iteration is superior by far, but this being a Hemingway story, the jury's still out. Anyway. She wants to rescue the cat; he thinks doing so would be madness and offers a couple of far-fetched excuses. They argue. They don't reach an agreement, and he gets his way – when there's a draw, inertia always trumps action – and the cat stays on the street. She cries a bit. They lie down on opposite sides of the bed, back to back.

I doubt I've told the story right. The beauty or practicality of the iceberg theory, as some people call it, is that you can change the surface of a story – the metaphorical tip of the iceberg – without changing the overall meaning. The story underneath this piece by Hemingway is so plain you've surely worked it out by now: the cat is the child the couple will never have.

Story A in our case – the tip of the iceberg – had to do with money: we were travelling to the south of France for work. Saying it was about money also establishes that it was about our various literary aspirations, given that modern-day authors are always in pursuit of financial stability, a thing impossible to find. Yet, our story could also be seen as just another episode in an overarching narrative that existed in Spain at the time, which made it so that young men and women were forced to choose between three options. Namely, spending the summer mixing drinks at some beach bar on the Mediterranean coast, moving to London to make sandwiches or look after some adorable brat and – theoretically – learn English, or harvesting grapes in the south of France. Option three most aligned with our interests, since it would also help us meet several of the demands placed on young middle-class men back then:

being lean and tanned, doing some form of manual labour (this is key, as it adds a whiff of social legitimacy to the resumé of any middle-aged professor or lawyer – the cliché being 'I too lived through tough times and had no choice but to work hard'), being financially solvent, etc. In a way, harvesting grapes would allow us to cultivate a future, or story for the future, but most of all (for me at least, or the person I was then), it was a volatile, hazy, ill-defined thing that we coined in the word *experience*.

Experience, we all know, is the *sine qua non* for creating literature. While I may not subscribe to the belief myself, the fact remains that this truism has permeated every literary decalogue in the field. Bolaño, for example – reading Bolaño being one of the unwritten commandments – declared that 'a short-story writer should be brave' and dive in headfirst. Piglia claimed his lifestyle defined his literary style. Augusto Monterroso urged young writers to 'make the most of every disadvantage, whether insomnia, imprisonment, or poverty; the first gave us Baudelaire, the second Silvio Pellico, and the third all your writer friends; avoid sleeping like Homer, living easily like Byron, or making as much money as Bloy.' (I've always thought that last one should be 'Bioy' – although, unlike Léon Bloy, Bioy Casares didn't so much 'make' money as *have* money.) With time and the proliferation of notes I jotted down in journals, diaries, and on scraps of paper, I developed my own decalogue of decalogues about experience as literary capital:

I. A short-story writer should be brave. Drop everything and dive in headfirst.

II. Make the most of every disadvantage, whether insomnia, imprisonment, or poverty; the first gave us Baudelaire, the second Silvio Pellico, and the third all your writer friends; avoid sleeping like Homer, living easily like Byron, or making as much money as Bloy.

III. Remember that writing isn't for cowards, but also that being brave isn't the same as not feeling afraid; being brave is feeling afraid and sticking it out, taking charge, going all in.

IV. Don't start writing poetry unless you've opened your eyes underwater, unless you've screamed underwater with your eyes wide open. Also, don't start writing poetry unless you've burned your fingers, unless you've put them under the hot water tap and said, 'Ahhh! This is much better than not getting burned at all.'

V. Be in love with your own life.

VI. What sets a novelist apart is having a unique worldview as well as something to say about it. So try living a little first. Not just in books or in bars, but out there, in real life. Wait until you've been scarred by the world, until it has left its mark.

VII. Try living abroad.

VIII. You've got to fuck a great many women / beautiful women / [...] / drink more and more beer / [...] attend the racetrack at least once.

IX. You've got to sell your heart, your strongest reactions, not the little minor things that only touch you lightly, the little experiences that you might tell at dinner.

X. People in a novel, not skilfully constructed characters, must be projected from the writer's assimilated experience, from his knowledge, from his head, from his heart, and from all there is of him.

The writers behind this advice – in strict disorder – are: Javier Cercas, Arturo Pérez-Reverte, Jack Kerouac, Ernest Hemingway, Paul Auster, Roberto Bolaño, Charles Bukowski, Hernán Casciari, F. Scott Fitzgerald, and Augusto Monterroso. (Exercise: draw a line between each author and his advice.) As might be expected, all ten authors are men. In our culture, entrepreneurship, a spirit for adventure, and self-advertising are qualities reserved to the male species. It's not for nothing that sex workers have been tainted as 'public women,' as opposed to 'private women,' who are 'good women.'

If you think about it, the fact that these rules exist at all is evidence of a loss. During the Middle Ages it was possible to sing ballads about the end of experience and

– more importantly – *from* the end of experience: i.e., prison. I'm talking about 'The Prisoner's Ballad,' which begins 'in May, it was in May, when the weather is warm,' and (in its most famous iteration) tells a story in sixteen verses about a man who knows when it's night and when it's day thanks to the little bird that visits him like clockwork, until it is eventually slain by an archer. The ballad in question could easily have been written by someone with no real experience, since it doesn't narrate experience so much as a human being's primal experience: an awareness of solar cycles. Had a speaker not been implied in the language we could have posited that another animal species altogether had written the ballad, maybe even a sunflower. Though the experience itself is unfamiliar, the ballad gives us a glimpse into a lifetime of sorrow and joy by way of its sparing description of a prison cell and a bird. The difference between us and the author is crucial: he believes everything stands for something deeper, that his shallow account of two or three details conceals the same ulterior reality as the fourteen thousand verses of the *Divine Comedy*. He doesn't go to the bother of describing the prison, or identifying the narrator with the author, or adding any depth whatsoever to the scene because he knows the depth is already there. And despite all this, he still makes us feel something.

In a way, every literary decalogue tells a writer's hypothetical future. According to the iceberg theory, my decadecalogue or metadecalogue should conceal an underwater mountain, and it does: it presumes certain experiences are more valuable than others. During our current phase of late-stage capitalism, we know that the stuff life is made of (time or the memory of a time that may or may not have passed) has – much like everything else – become a commodity. Travelling around Latin America, Thailand, or Canada; living in New York City, Madrid, or Paris because 'there are things going on there'; squandering our youth in the quest for a body that's always beyond reach – these are all the minor consequences of applying economic theory to a new type of commodity: free time (a perverse expression by and of itself as it presupposes the existence of a time that isn't free and belongs to somebody else). The investment is the price of a plane ticket, or rent, or a dozen pints of beer; the return is the optimization of a period of time that would have passed anyway had you spent it reading, ingesting, or socializing. It's not about maximizing that strange thing we call happiness so much as leading a *better life*. The people with the worst lives are the poor, who spend less and therefore barely move the machine of experience, who are always deader, greyer, harder to understand, less human.

Our underwater stories had a lot to do with that. Take me, for example. I was travelling because I knew I would write about our trip one day. Not like I am now, but the way – as I said before – I intend to avoid in these pages. Writing like a writer. It took six years for the corpse of fiction – which has been rotting inside me ever since those long months in the south of France – to turn to dust before I could tell the story of what really happened.

I don't know what my friends' underwater stories – their icebergs – were. I figure Ernesto was trying to make amends for his original sin: being born rich under capitalism. He didn't need the money we would make harvesting grapes, that's for sure. I have a hunch Alejandro's motivations were the same as mine. G, on the other hand, did need the money and may have been fleeing the burden of earning a steady living by turning his first post-graduation summer into a teenage holiday not unlike a return to Paradise Lost. Or maybe he was just trying to get away from his family. Speculating about what others are thinking may be at odds with my promise to hew to the truth. Though isn't it equally true that I tried to get into their heads that summer (isn't that something we do – try to get into other people's heads to avoid being in our own – all the time?)? In any event, since this text is a book – inasmuch as everything is a book – we'll just have to infer my friends' motivations from their behaviour, from what I narrate. For the time being, let me just stress that none of us were travelling for money, hence our insistence that money was our only reason for travelling. Money – we all know – makes it possible to talk about things without addressing them directly; bypassing that intermediary would have been considered obscene. That's why we didn't discuss our real motivations until the very end, when everything became unbearable and there was no reason to pretend any more.

III.
LOS COMBATIENTES,
OR THE FIGHTERS

We were happy on the road, and happiness doesn't abide by the rules of literature. Nor can it be narrated. Though maybe it can be summed up with a phrase like this one: 'We drove across Spain in one go, stopping only so Alejandro and I could take turns behind the wheel. Neither Ernesto nor G have driving licences.' And that's it.

The motorway signs were already littered with the names of French towns by the time we got lost. Thanks to my dad being Algerian, I spoke French better than the rest of the crew and should have been the one to ask for directions. But by that point in the trip, I was experiencing a strange mix of joy, exhaustion, and Stendhal syndrome. On the one hand, the French countryside is achingly beautiful. On the other, it's covered in a variety of grasses, which I'm allergic to, and I'd been driving for longer than advisable. The last thing I remember before waking up in Aire-sur-l'Adour is Ernesto – the only other one of us with a basic grasp of French – walking toward a middle-aged couple in a tiny gas station in the middle of nowhere. The sight of Ernesto walking away from us, his slender figure cut by the sun and circled by shades of yellow and green, by grass and trees and flowers, while I drifted off to sleep.

Memories of dreams work in mysterious ways. I can barely remember what I dreamed last night, yet I have a clear memory of a random dream from six years ago. Also, sometimes I can't tell if a memory is real or just a dream. In the short space of my nap, I dreamed I was strolling through the countryside and soaking up nature with all five of my senses. While I wandered, it started getting dark. Suddenly I felt a rifle against my shoulder and realized I wasn't on a stroll but fighting in the battle for the independence of southern France, which in the dream was – and this is something I can get behind – a legitimate territory of the Algerian people. I saw three French soldiers walking through the trees in the faint twilight and was seized by a terrible doubt: to kill them or to run. I couldn't remember the orders I'd been given and was neither ethical nor inherently strategic enough to settle that internal dilemma.

G woke me up just as we were entering Aire-sur-l'Adour. I realize that the name Aire-sur-l'Adour is quite jarring and pretty unbearable to anyone with even a vague sense of aesthetics. If this were a piece of short fiction, I might have changed it. But it isn't, so I'm leaving it as is, just as I have the names of my friends. So, we were driving into Aire-sur-l'Adour. Ernesto and Álex were pointing at things out the window and cheerfully talking about a Vietnamese restaurant they'd seen near the town limits and the possibility of commemorating our first paycheque there.

Arriving somewhere unfamiliar tends to awaken an ancestral fear. You don't know if you're going to find shelter, a cave or an overhang to start a fire under, maybe a cozy house, or – in our case – a campground or hostel. Aire-sur-l'Adour tacitly conveyed a warm sense of welcome, the promise that a quaint town with gable roofs and pristine streets where polished, smiling people read the daily news on the sunny terraces of beautiful cafés couldn't possibly be hostile.

A couple of questions later, we were on our way to *le camping*. Les Ombrages de l'Adour occupied a substantial piece of land beside the river. Access to the campground was past a large building, a cross between a bull ring and a missile-launch facility whose purpose we could never figure out and that we thought of as a beacon signalling the position of the campground. A friendly-looking guy came out to meet us. He was cheerful and lean, in flip-flops and a weird fisherman's hat. We said hello and asked about the rate; he insisted on showing us around first. We could tell that Aire-sur-l'Adour was teeming with seasonal workers and that it would be easy enough to settle on a price. We liked *le camping*. True, we hadn't gone through the usual motions of people looking for a place to rent or buy, instead letting ourselves be swayed by inertia, the result of accumulated exhaustion and the longing for somewhere to drop our bags. The fact that the campground boasted a playground was proof that it was a wholesome place – and that we didn't belong. Naturally, I didn't say this aloud.

At long last, he took us to the welcome booth to discuss pricing. We didn't have tents, which meant we'd have to rent a stationary caravan (as Ernesto called them), i.e. a caravan with the wheels taken off. We mentioned we had mats and an air mattress and didn't mind sleeping outside – there was no need for a caravan. The guy almost conceded but then his wife locked eyes with him while smiling and shaking her head no. A discussion unfolded in the claustrophobic booth. Somehow the woman had extricated our passports from us and, as we negotiated with her husband, she wrote down names and figures, all while still smiling and shaking her head. The guy managed to persuade us that we needed a caravan. We were used to staying in hostels around Latin America – and in so doing acquiring *experience* – and for some reason had assumed *le camping* would have a communal kitchen, which it did not. Meaning, we'd need a caravan for kitchen access, a fridge, and a power source. As soon as we gave in, the woman noted that there were four of us and only two cots per vehicle, so we would need two caravans. This time we stood our ground. One caravan would do; we could take turns sleeping outside. The woman was wise enough to glean from the pearls of sweat around our eyes that we couldn't afford two caravans and so eventually gave in. Three further discussions ensued: about the deposit for the power supply, the daily rate, and the method of payment. In all three cases we managed to meet more or less halfway between what they wanted and what we were willing to fork out. The ancestral fear of not finding shelter had lifted: we had somewhere to drop our bags. We sat beside the caravan – on beach chairs, tree stumps, the cajón, and on the ground – to celebrate. Álex broke out the Manchego cheese and Maria biscuits left over from the road trip. Meanwhile, Ernesto inspected the caravan – which turned out to be minuscule – and surrounding areas. There was no hot water in the shower, he discovered, but we didn't care. We were full of optimism, enough to treat the cheese and biscuits as a full meal. A couple of minor details weren't about to deflate us. Once we finished eating – which took no time at all – we walked to the riverside (jumping over the boundary fence that marked the end of the campground) and chatted a bit while drinking the few remaining lukewarm beers from the road trip. G told us about a girl he went to bed with a long time ago in Madrid. When he'd taken off her clothes, he'd noticed she was completely waxed – crotch, armpits, and legs – and been turned off. G had slept with other women who were waxed before her, so his reaction didn't make sense. He asked us what we made of it. Ernesto posited that something about that girl in particular had probably turned him off, some detail G couldn't call to mind right then. G pointed out there were other women after her (including his current girlfriend) whom he hadn't managed to have sex with when waxed. Ernesto asserted that trauma can ripple into the future and sometimes even the past, like waves in a pond – then he threw a stone into the Adour River, ruining the metaphor. Alejandro asked if G and the girl ever got round to fucking. G's response was ambiguous: he did what he could with his hands, and she got G to come in her mouth (fellatio, he claimed, had helped him dissociate). Feeling the need to weigh in, I told them about a dream I'd had. I was in a park. A neighbourhood park in the outskirts of a city that could have been big or small. My friend Fran was tossing rocks at a wall with the word BLOW on it in big, capital letters. Fran was aiming for the letter O. I watched the rock and thought that if he managed to hit the O off the wall, then it would just read BL W. If my dream were a screenplay and the screenwriter had been asked to explain the plot, they might have said something along the lines of 'psychomotricity,' 'proprioception,' and 'body awareness.' I didn't think Fran had the necessary skills: in my dream an act as simple as tossing a rock fell under the category of 'superhuman feat.' I stared at my fingers and thought about all the micro-movements entailed in throwing a rock, about how you had to let go at just the right moment for it to land where you wanted it to. I pictured all my fingers opening at the same time, in sync with my arm, and knew deep down that throwing a rock was an impossible task, that striking the letter O belonged to the realm of implausibility. I asked Fran to let me have a go. In the dream I was aware of the fact that in some world I could only hazily remember – and despite all proof to the contrary – throwing a rock was considered straightforward. Fran gave me permission, and I bent my knees and went for it. The first time I couldn't even let go. The fifth time I let go, but the rock fell behind my heels after bopping me on the shoulder. The sixth time – perhaps in the context of this dream there was no such thing as learning – I couldn't let go of the rock either.

Alejandro interrupted to ask if I kept trying. I said I tried at least another twenty times, until it felt like agony and I woke up. Ernesto said nothing; he was peeling branches, tossing them in the river, and watching them drift away. G asked what my story had to do with his but then immediately got to thinking and said that what our two stories had in common was a sense of defamiliarization or estrangement, which the Russian formalists – he said – referred to as *ostranenie*. '*Ostranenie*,' he explained, 'was created with a clear political intent, like deconstruction.' I expressed my doubts about this affirmation, given that to me *ostranenie* was a purely analytical concept; G replied that in either case both procedures could be highly transformative. Alejandro asked why. G explained that just as seeing a urinal in a museum compels us to consider that object under a new regime of light and darkness, seeing a police officer in uniform in the middle of the desert – for example – could strip him of his aura of power and allow us – he claimed – 'to see the emperor naked.' 'Okay, but,' I interjected, 'the reason defamiliarization works is anthropological; we're encouraged to flatten difference, to seek out similarities in our thinking. It functions on a deeper level than politics.' G voiced the unwavering conviction that nothing is deeper than politics and added that even if my theory was right, it only gave more credence to *ostranenie* and in no way detracted from its transformative potential. I conceded. Ernesto – who was getting a bit bored – noted that we were out of beer and should probably drive to a supermarket before it got late. 'In France,' he said, 'people have dinner at six and it's already four-thirty.'

We went grocery shopping. We were shocked by the number of chain supermarkets in France with footholds in Spain, like Alcampo and Carrefour. We drove past an Intermarché and a Géant Casino. Our shopping list might actually be a perfect outline for a chronicle of our time in Aire-sur-l'Adour, one composed of nutritional values, saturated fats, carbohydrates, and animal products; a tale, in short, that Schopenhauer and other physiognomists would have found much more interesting than the one I'm telling. It would begin like this: twenty-four six-packs of hot dogs (the cheapest kind), five twenty-four-packs of store-brand beer, twelve kilos of pasta, twelve kilos of rice, fifteen frozen pizza doughs, five trays of cold ham, twenty-five cans of prepared food (lentils, beans with chorizo, and a revolting mixture of meats called *le cassoulet*), six giant variety packs of potato chips, ten two-litre bottles of Coca-Cola, twenty cartons of milk, seven trays of ground meat for the pasta, a massive and comically cheap bag of shredded cheese that turned out to have no flavour whatsoever, salt, sugar, multiple boxes of store-brand biscuits, ten jars of instant coffee, and thirty-six tubs of yogurt. The piece would proceed with annotations like 'Monday, 22 July: for breakfast we had two boxes of biscuits, a litre of milk, and two pots of coffee' (better yet would be to cite the quantities in grams or millilitres – better, needless to say, for Schopenhauer). Every character would be a cashier or dinner guest, and the story would end after two months, during which the sole obstacles were a spot of constipation and diarrhea. Every day would be as interesting as the last and there would exist no such thing as chronological hierarchy. Yet, in our story some days are more important than others, and at the end of our first in Aire-sur-l'Adour, after the trip to the supermarket, we did little or nothing.

We woke up at nine the next morning and went to get breakfast at the trendy café we'd seen on our way into town. It turned out to be too expensive, so we headed back to *le camping* and had warm milk with instant coffee and biscuits. The flavour fluctuated between wet cardboard and cork, which prompted us to add more sugar than usual and feel exhilarated for a while. Ernesto clocked what was going on and rolled a joint to help us come down. The Belgian family in the adjoining campsite shot us dirty looks. The mother grabbed her daughter by the arm and stormed off to the welcome booth. The daughter was about our age, and we gawked at her as she retreated. The father – whom I'd been watching out of the corner of my eye – gave us a murderous stare and settled his 160-kilo frame into a plastic chair, returning his attention to his laptop. Álex passed the joint to G, who passed it to me, and I handed it back to Ernesto. Neither G nor I smoked that time. He'd developed a very legitimate fear of weed in Mexico, convinced it had the potential to awaken a latent schizophrenia; I just wanted to be fresh for our interview with Élodie, the woman who'd be employing us on the basis of a recommendation from a French *amie* of Ernesto's mom (the woman, I believe, had taught him how to ride horses or something – it doesn't actually matter).

Ernesto finished smoking the joint and we got up. We had to go to a place called Association Solidarité Travail (AST) – just like that, without determiners or prepositions. Álex was in the caravan fetching his harmonica and the rest of us were collecting our things when we saw the owner of *le camping* striding in our direction. This is when it dawned on us that our campsite was revolting: strewn with cigarette butts and empty beer cans, while the air mattress – where I'd spent the night in a Decathlon sleeping bag – was covered in leaves and a brownish liquid that was a mix of dew and some coffee I'd spilled. The scattered cups and tins of food didn't help. The campground owner was wearing a similar outfit to the day before (like a fisherman adrift on the moon) and the same imperishable smile. He said he wanted to talk to us (now that I think of it, he probably said he *needed* to talk to us). I pretended to translate while telling the others to start leaving like they were in a hurry. The owner of *le camping* tried to stop them but managed only to keep me for a few seconds. He said something about his long-lost youth, about how he too had been young or whatever, but he spoke so fast I had trouble parsing his words. I promised to talk to him about the springtime of his life later that evening, then left with feigned urgency. I walked past the Belgian woman and her daughter on my way out and greeted them with a smile.

AST was in the centre of Aire. It consisted of a single room, a kind of office space devoid of decorations, with stacks of paper all over. Behind the counter, a chubby French woman with a big smile was chatting with a Moroccan man in his thirties. He was dark-skinned, dark-haired, and terribly thin, too gaunt and bony for his age. We found out later that his name was Muhammad, and he was from Fez. He had black, sunken eyes that looked straight through you, and a hooked Arab nose. He spoke very little and knew – or perhaps couldn't help it – how to make people cower in his presence. His lips were thin, and a scar yarned his mouth, where some of his teeth were missing.

The fat woman greeted us far too effusively, all while giggling and squealing. Her first words to us were addressed to G, whom she asked for a glass of water from one of those plastic dispensers used in First World countries to keep the temperature cool. G didn't understand a word she said, of course, and the woman – down whose face and neck rolled large pearls of sweat, despite the loud fan pointed right at her – asked if we spoke French. I said we did, while Ernesto, being more practical, went to the water cooler to get the fat woman what she had asked for. The

Moroccan guy seemed uncomfortable. Maybe he didn't like people standing behind him, or we rubbed him the wrong way. In any case, he kept scratching the back of his neck and glancing at us over his shoulder. He quickly signed something and closed a folder, holding it out to the woman while mumbling some implausible, unnecessary excuse. He eyed us with a mix of hatred and distrust, then got up and left without saying goodbye.

The woman found the Moroccan man's behaviour totally normal. She introduced herself. Her name was Élodie and she was in charge of AST. She took the glass Ernesto held out for her and asked what she could do for us. *Que puis-je faire pour vous?* Álex and G smiled and nodded, an attitude they kept up throughout the rest of the conversation. Feeling protective of his mother's friend's reputation, Ernesto had made us 'dress nice,' which had translated into everyone but him looking patently ridiculous. We'd promised to keep our composure and make a good impression, so I stifled the urge to laugh at the sight of Álex with his mohawk and button-down shirt and G in swimming trunks and dress shoes – borrowed from Ernesto, naturally – smiling and nodding like idiots as I explained to Élodie that we'd come to work the grape harvest, that we wanted to be part of *une équipe*, a squad – by then the heat, claustrophobia, and sugar high had got to me – that we'd rented a caravan at Les Ombrages campground but hadn't signed anything about a minimum-stay period so were free to leave at any time, much as it seemed like a great place, and well located too, that we could request references from the owner – we'd only been there a day but had picked up on a certain feeling (*le filín*, I said) – though obviously we'd prefer somewhere with guaranteed room and board, even if it was docked from our wages, and so long, it goes without saying, as the price was reasonable – they could dock our room or our board but not both. I fell quiet at the sight of Ernesto staring at me wide-eyed while Álex and G had stopped nodding along to look at me. I'd been spouting everything I knew about the grape harvest – which wasn't a lot – while the woman erratically jotted down a few details. What I mean by 'erratically' is that she didn't write anything when I made an important point but at seemingly random junctures, as if she had decided to note down only my prepositions and adverbs. I leaned forward in my seat hoping to catch her writing 'to, to, to, for, in, of,' for example, or 'well, quickly, obviously, very' but saw nothing, and Ernesto pulled me back by the shoulder. We were all sweating buckets and pining for Élodie's fan. Meanwhile, I had started feeling a bit under the weather, almost feverish. In that moment of silence, Ernesto informed me I'd been 'raving like a lunatic' and went on to give Élodie a more structured account of our story. He talked about Paule – his mother's friend – about horses and the grape harvest. Paule's name – which should have acted as a sort of magic word, judging by the expectations created during our road trip – had no effect. Élodie declared she didn't know anyone called Paule, certainly not *that* Paule. Ernesto wrapped up his story feeling less confident – the situation was incredibly surreal – while Élodie went on taking notes without rhyme or reason. As soon as Ernesto was done, the woman looked at us and said, 'You do know there isn't going to be a grape harvest this summer, right?'

Ernesto and I looked at each other in shock. Élodie chuckled in a way that was truly disarming, circumstances notwithstanding. G and Álex must have picked up on something because they once again stopped smiling and nodding. All of a sudden, I saw the scene from the outside: having driven across Spain for the grape harvest, four guys in improbable clothes sit in a kind of post-apocalyptic cubicle with temperatures of circa 120°C only to partially discover – since two of them still don't quite know what's going on – that there is no grape harvest and no work and that they may have to turn round and drive straight back home. I couldn't help myself: I burst out laughing. Ernesto shot me a withering glare. G and Álex looked even more confused and gazed at each other as if one of them might have the answer, or at least part of the answer, that the other lacked. Élodie, meanwhile, laughed with me and then proceeded to explain that torrential rainfall had spoiled the vineyards, making the grape harvest smaller and later than usual, October with any luck. *Ne vous tracassez pas*, she said, or *ne vous inquiétez pas* or something of the kind, I think, and then informed us there were plenty of other jobs – like *les poulets, les canards*, or *les cailles* – in need of strapping young men like us. Of course, these other jobs weren't as well remunerated as the grape harvest, but we had come to work, *non? Mais si*, we had indeed come to work and would at the very least need to defray the cost of the gas we'd burned through to get there. *Tout à fait*, Élodie said with understanding. *Tout à fait*, and then she handed us some forms.

Ernesto called time out. His French was decent but also kind of rusty and he wasn't sure if we were driving back to Spain, taking a job called *les cailles*, or going to jail; the situation was starting to get the better of him. So he called a time-out, which Élodie granted with a smile that we took as a beam of approval, though we would come to recognize it as her standard response to any and all input. We went outside to smoke. I think that was the first cigarette I had in my life. We filled G and Álex in on what had happened, and they both shrugged. *So long as there's work* … they said. Every now and then, between drags, I peeked inside and was surprised to see Élodie staying exactly where she was. She could write, answer the phone, and reach for the ledger without ever abandoning her sphere of action. It occurred to me that if she moved too much she might melt. Now that I think of it, I'm not sure I ever saw her outside that chair.

When we walked back in, Élodie was on the phone. In the meantime, we filled out the forms. We handed the pages to her when she hung up, and she glanced at them with complete indifference. In a surge of patriotism, Ernesto asked if she was surprised that four Spaniards had come to harvest grapes in France. Her response wasn't ill-intentioned: No, she said, she was used to receiving plenty of people from Spain, well – *bon* – from Spain but also Romania, Morocco, Algeria, Portugal, *et cetera*. Which made us an *et cetera*, a surplus. That day we learned that we were but the *et cetera* of Europe. That truth – which may seem obvious today – was a revelation at the time, and I doubt any of us will forget Élodie's ample face as she handed down that sentence. The woman interrupted our silence to note a mistake in Álex's form: he'd written that he had an undergraduate degree. I told her it wasn't a mistake, that I had a degree too and – a lie – we had wanted to harvest grapes to save up for the master's programs we'd enrolled in for the following year. For every response I tendered, Élodie returned a look of deep sadness: that of a father from blue-collar Vallecas who, when his twelve-year-old son declares he wants to be an architect or an astronaut or the president, pats him on the shoulder while weighing up how much he'll need the boy to work full time at the fruit store once he turns sixteen, because the household has a mortgage and electricity and credit-card bills to pay and because time – from legal working age, sometimes even sooner – is money; a look, in a nutshell that can either curb or crush the future and lasted no longer than a second before Élodie regained her composure and went back, as ever, to smiling.

She said we would reconvene the next day to discuss our wages and duties. We couldn't figure out whether we ought to say yes or no, so in the end we just nodded. I remember she shook hands with us one by one, never moving from her seat, and that we spent the rest of the day smoking weed on the little bridge over the Adour (*le pont*, le bridge, le pón; it's time I mentioned that we rechristened every single thing we came across: le campeen, la vwature, le traveye, and – though these would come later – le poolé, le mayze, and la joorné were all magic words we used to banish the unyielding present). We waited until dark before sneaking back into *le camping*, side-stepping the owner and therefore the conversation we'd managed to wriggle out of earlier that morning. We had a dinner of tinned food – by then Ernesto had earned himself a title he would have no trouble holding on to: being the only person who could bring himself to eat *le cassoulet* – and went to sleep.

IV.
CHRONICLE OF A
DEATH FORETOLD

I always assumed telling the story of what actually happened would be easier than writing fiction (after all, reality is more painstaking than even the most exhaustive inventions), but I'm beginning to notice that's not the case. Reality is under no obligation to be interesting – neither is memory – while literature is. I can't seem to clear enough room in my memories to make space for mystery and surprise. True, I could shuffle them around, but doing so would be untruthful in its own way. I believe Borges followed a similar thought process when he wrote 'Funes the Memorious,' a short story about a guy who can't forget and therefore can't think (let alone invent). Borges's story – like all good fantasy stories – isn't concerned with rigour. A while ago I tried my hand at fixing 'Funes the Memorious' and wrote a piece of flash fiction called 'Ireneo's Memory,' which later won a prize. Here it is, from memory:

 Ireneo's memory was vast and exhaustive. It all started the day he fell off a wall. When he woke up, he recalled everything in perfect detail. The next moment he remembered that he remembered, and the moment after that he remembered that he remembered, and so he remained, trapped in an event, a memory, in a compact, anodyne, infinite moment.

Borges, as we all know, wasn't big on realism. He'd have laughed at the quote by that French author – Aragon, I think he was called, Louis Aragon – who said something along the lines of 'No one knows more than I the sacrifice and surrender needed to make literary realism' (what a lovely instance of the verb *make*). In fact, 'The Aleph' is itself a joke *about* or *against* literary realism and the realist writer personified by Carlos Argentino Daneri. I'm not trying to eschew Borges's critiques. Then again, I'm not a realist writer. First, because I'm not a writer and hate to be called one; second, because the suffix *-ist* always implies a degree of artifice.

I remember being Borgesian at one point (nowadays I'm just an admirer). I also remember believing that some books help us write better. Before starting a story, I always reached for one on the shelf. Depending on what I wanted to write, on the genre and tone, I might pull out *Ficciones* or *The Savage Detectives* or *The Past* or *Historia Argentina* or *Fever Dream* or *Pequeña flor*. Those and a handful of other volumes were the ones that inspired me, or better still, saturated me. They weren't my top ten so much as books that made me want to write (what a feeling, wanting to write) and warmed up my brain (*warm up* in the sense of a runner who limbers up their muscles before running the biggest race of their lives). I would read a few lines, a few pages, a few chapters. Very rarely did I get hooked and stick with a book to the end, inhaling the entire thing in one sitting and forgetting I had set out to write at all. Usually I just immersed myself in the language, soaked it up, then started writing. The question now is: how do I write the plain truth? What should I read? There's no point in turning to non-fiction by the likes of Rodolfo Walsh or Truman Capote; as far as I can see, there's as much artifice in their work as in any other author's. Maybe they wrote their own truths. But as time and space shift, so do reading experiences. My argument collapses when it becomes clear that the only thing I can read is a piece of non-fiction written by me, and only while I'm writing it.

In France I kept a journal that I have little use for now, at least insofar as journals can be useful: as memory devices. Bad as my memory is, I will never forget that summer, no matter how hard I try. I've held on to that diary for two reasons. First, in that notebook – bound in yellow by a stranger, incidentally, at a squat house in Buenos Aires – there is a Munir who is no longer me and, I dare say, never was. The second reason is twofold: some of these journal entries spring to mind at moments that bear a passing resemblance to them. The trigger could be a baker puzzling over a coin or a butcher dropping a knife so that it lands smack in the middle of a chicken carcass. Small details that still prompt me to revisit past events or – better yet – how

I wrote about them. These unexpected connections led me to come up with a new game: instead of waiting for the trigger, I pick a random moment and find a comparable one in the diary. This is how the yellow notebook went from being a period of my life fixed on paper to a paper intervening in a period of my life (which I also fix on paper). I say 'paper' because I've always written by hand, though the medium stops having a role when I summon the journal to the present: by virtue of the game's repetitiveness, I've come to know the journal by heart. Every now and then I wonder what kind of self-destructive impulse compelled me to add to the memory of Aire-sur-l'Adour the memory of its memory or of its story. Come to think of it, I'm playing the game this very moment. Earlier, while reflecting on memory, I couldn't help recalling a journal entry from Tuesday, 16 July:

G, Alejandro, and I were talking about memory and the business of writing. Ernesto was in the caravan making coffee. What he was actually doing was staving off an inevitable dispute: he wants us to tidy the campsite, which – in his words – *looks like a pigsty*, because he's afraid we'll be kicked out if we don't. I'm the only one who has his back, albeit with minimal enthusiasm – ever since I started working in Aire-sur-l'Adour I do everything with minimal enthusiasm. Alejandro claims that *in current times* – bringing everything back to current times is a trait I admire in his thinking – writers don't need a good memory; sometimes it even gets in the way. G is smoking in silence. I say Funes would concur, but something about his reasoning doesn't sit right with me. He asks what, and G looks my way. It takes me a while to reply because I'm embarrassed, but in the end I admit to having a lot of insecurity around my bad memory (long-term; my short-term memory is exceptional). For a minute we all fall quiet. Ernesto walks out of the caravan holding a pot of coffee, looks around, and sits down with us. I tell them that the writers I admire – more than anything, it's the tacit confession that I want to be a writer that most embarrasses me – either have or had great memory: Piglia, Borges, Bolaño, etc. They also share a gift for the quick retort, a brilliant use of irony, and the witty, cutting note. G says all three are white and male. I'm not sure what he's implying – or rather I can think of several things he may be implying but struggle to zero in on a single one (I'm still struggling as I write this). Alejandro makes a point I find oddly comforting: he says that what all three have in common is success and a certain aptitude in the field – these are his exact words – but that the *field* has changed; we live in the age of Google, our Absolute Memory (he says it like that, capitalized), and in our day and age it's the nimble writer who will prevail, the writer who can fashion a persuasive argument out of a handful of facts, the *anti-Google*. I'm about to say you could use that same argument as a rebuttal, but I'm hypnotized by his apocalyptic tone and decide not to interrupt. G intervenes. He asks if Álex has read Byung-Chul Han. I take advantage of the fact that he can't reply – Ernesto just passed him a joint – and cut in again. Maybe I'm unconsciously jealous of these white men's fame. 'But,' I say, 'all I would need to reject that fame is knowing I've written a single memorable page. Even if I couldn't sign my name to it. It'd be enough to write one page like Borges.' It dawns on me that I've been sincere: the pleasure of good writing trumps the business of success. G says I'm being idealistic. He isn't wrong. And yet, I was being sincere.

I worry these reflections could serve literature as an entry point to my story. Yet, my elaborating on them here still counts as a form of sincerity, given that all my thinking is being done through that yellow notebook. Keeping a journal is a perilous thing, and we should be warned against it as children. In a way, fixing the past and referring back to that past means becoming enmeshed in the dense thicket of memory. Like the protagonist of my piece of flash fiction.

From now on I won't narrate events in the order they occurred. Things unfold in the margins of our lives, often long after they first happened. To the man who found out his wife was seeing his best friend behind his back, the many visits to their family home to help with the kids, or their occasional run-ins around the neighbourhood, don't actually take place until a long time after they first occurred (before then, they were just happy coincidences or polite interest in a friend's children). I've promised rigour, but rigour has no concern for order (at least the chronological kind, which is as arbitrary as any other).

To say the first three weeks were our best would be inexact, if not a flat-out lie. To say things only got worse from then on would be more precise and at the same time incredibly naive. I don't know how to order events to reveal their true meaning. For now, I will interlard journal entries (transcribed from memory) with as little commentary as possible.

Sunday, 7 July
Today is our first day of work. Élodie informed us that we get €10 an hour for day shifts and €13 an hour for nights. In France – it seems – night starts at midnight on the dot and day starts at six. No one has explained yet what 'la chamba' – as G calls it, having picked up the word in Mexico – consists of. Élodie said it's different every time and someone at the site will fill us in. I asked her if the French state didn't recognize double time for employees who work Sundays, but she acted like she didn't understand and started talking with Muhammad, who was waiting at the office. I interrupted their conversation a little aggressively – I haven't been sleeping much on account of the heat – and repeated the question. For a moment her everlasting smile fell (we call her the Cheshire cat) only to immediately return and for her to explain with her pudgy lips that yes, of course it does, *mon cher*, that we wouldn't be working on Sunday but on Monday, since the shift started at midnight. On the one hand her answer bugged us, but on the other we were excited to find out what we

would be doing and – I may as well admit it – work for the first time in our lives. Plus, the pay was decent compared to Spain, so we just shut up and left. On our way out, the fat woman suddenly remembered something and told me that we should meet outside AST at twelve thirty.

Monday, 8 July
I'm writing this on a short break before heading back to work. It's 4.30 p.m. and we haven't eaten yet. We just got home from the grocery shop. I have this paradoxical urge to memorialize last night as the worst night of my life. As it happens, I haven't slept a wink and can't say for sure if night has in fact ended, even though daylight is what's stopping me from getting any rest. We're all dead tired, and the others are trying to nap despite the mosquitos and the heat and the humidity from the river, but I know there's no point in trying and, besides, I'd rather stay up and write down what happened last night – before I forget anything, even the smallest detail.

We arrive at AST at the scheduled hour and find El Moro there – we call Muhammad 'the Moor'; the guys keep insisting I talk to him in Arabic but he creeps me out and I don't really want to. We say hello and he ignores us – it's like we don't exist. The man is ridiculously cold, though the scar on his face is decidedly unridiculous, which makes him terrifyingly cold. Ernesto rolls a joint, then puts it away as the other workers start showing up. They're Manuel – his mother is Spanish – and Fabrice. Fabrice is tall and sturdy and smiles constantly. Not the way the owner of *le camping* and Élodie smile, but in earnest. We're going in his car. Muhammad gives him directions, then disappears. It still isn't clear to me what El Moro's role is at AST.

Manuel hogs everyone's attention on the drive. He talks to us about Spain, though he knows next to nothing about it. He has a rare talent for piecing together an entire country out of four or five random facts. He talks nineteen to the dozen. Fabrice and I are in the front, and Manuel and the other three are squeezed into the back seat. I'm sure the reason I have the honour of riding shotgun has to do with my being the fattest of the crew, but since obesity makes people uncomfortable, we all pretend I'm in the front seat because my French is better. Halfway through the drive Ernesto asks Fabrice if he can smoke weed in his car, and Fabrice nods and smiles. G and Alejandro stop pretending they understand what Manuel is saying to them, and he acts offended – jokingly, I think – then, for our sakes, starts mixing his native French with what he thinks he knows of Spanish. Now no one in the car can understand him. I get the feeling Fabrice is driving over the speed limit but don't want to ask. I talk to him for a bit while Manuel tries communicating with the others in the back. Fabrice tells me a few things about the area and shows me a photo of his wife and kids, a boy and girl of four and seven. I tell him they're adorable, and I really mean it.

When we reach our destination, we realize there is no farm. Fabrice makes a phone call and Manuel reassures us everything's okay, that we're a little early because Fabrice was driving 150 kilometres an hour when the speed limit is 60. This time I ask why, but before Manuel can say anything we see a man coming toward us up a slope: first his head, then the flashlight in his hand. Manuel smiles, opens the trunk, and starts getting changed. We look at each other. Manuel asks if we brought any work clothes. Ernesto says no, so Manuel asks if Élodie told us what to bring. We say no, and he gets pissed off. He calls her a fucking cow and a cheat, and Fabrice tells him to cool down. He says a couple of kind words, then lends each of us a pair of latex gloves (minus G, who had the forethought to bring his grandfather's beekeeping gloves, though not the coveralls or boots) and suggests we work barefoot. We think he's joking, so we laugh. He shrugs, waves at the man with the flashlight, and we start making our way downhill. We can see the farm now. It's made up of five or six long warehouses with corrugated steel roofs. The poor animals must be boiling.

The work we're doing is called *l'attrapage*, a subcategory of what we refer to as 'le poolé' (*les poulets*). The gig involves going into the warehouses, grabbing some chickens and sticking them into a sort of wheeled cage. The guy we're following around – the farmer, it turns out – validates our manliness or underscores his own by saying he's glad we didn't bring gloves because this way the hens can rough up our hands with their beaks. He shows us his, calloused up to the forearms. He says he always helps out the *saisonniers* but this time he didn't bring appropriate clothing. I tell him I can lend him mine, but the joke falls flat or maybe nobody gets it.

The work is just what the man described, except with a million additional obscure details. The first thought I have when he opens the warehouse is that we ourselves are one of the *poor animals* whose situation I'd mourned when I first saw the farm. Nights in this place aren't cool to start, but the corrugated steel roof and the chickens exacerbate the heat, raising the temperature inside to approximately 400°C or higher. I say *chickens* because it's a literal translation of *poulets*, but they're actually aggressively fat hens, doubtless the result of some genetic modification. We're ankle-deep in chicken shit and the smell is unbearable. All we hear before the guy turns on the spotlights are a few scattered clucks, but as soon as the cold lights snap on, the birds go berserk. That's when we realize we can barely walk for all the chickens in the warehouse. Manuel instantly transforms. He yells at us to hurry – the chickens are fleeing to the corners, crushing and smothering each other. The farmer undergoes a similar transformation; he yanks at my arm, forcing me to help him stick a chicken into one of the wheeled cages. I struggle on account of my wide skater shoes, a pair of Zoo Yorks that keep getting sucked into the excrement. We move the cage and hear the crunching of bones. Manuel is hyperkinetic, which leads to a few failed attempts. Fabrice is slow and efficient. His technique is flawless and he navigates the space as if he were somewhere else. He grabs the chickens by their feet, three with his right hand and two with his left. As soon as they're upside down, the chickens surrender. Fabrice throws them in the cage five at a time. Álex and G are as disoriented as the chickens, and Ernesto is staring down at his arm, which is bleeding from various points. The farmer gives me a hard shove and tells me to get to work. Despite the millions of micro-feathers floating in the air and making it hard for me to breathe – I have asthma – I crouch down and try to copy Fabrice. I grab two chickens with my left hand and two with my right (three is too many). They peck me a few times, but that's the least of my concerns. The only thing that matters is for this hell to end as soon as possible so that I – like Fabrice – can be somewhere else.

It takes us an hour and a half to catch six hundred chickens. The four of us – the ones without safety goggles – are in tears. But it turns out we were too slow; the farmer says we're done for the day, that he's going to call up another, faster (and therefore cheaper) crew. He tells us he'd prepped another two warehouses for us but that he can't work with people this inept and ill-equipped. Fabrice tells us not to worry, it's Élodie's fault for not warning us; Manuel makes no effort to hide his rage. Because of us he's losing money and that's all he cares about.

No one talks on the drive back. Fabrice and Manuel get changed, then shove their clothes into sealed bags in the trunk of the car. Needless to say, the four of us don't have bags or a change of clothes, so we climb into the car filth and all – it isn't long before the stench is overwhelming.

Fabrice rolls down the windows. I apologize for ruining his car, but he says not to worry, he washes it every day; it's part of the job. I notice him going way over the speed limit again, and again can't bring myself to mention it. Besides, the fresh air on my face is a godsend. We make it back to Aire at 5:30 a.m.

Fabrice drops us at AST, and we have to walk down to *le camping*. We get there around six. The Belgians are already up and about, preparing for some kind of family excursion. They watch us wide-eyed and, when we're fifteen metres or so away, cover their noses. Alejandro says we just lost any chance we had with the daughter; we haven't talked in hours and his voice comes out hoarse. No one laughs. We're all thinking the same thing, that the sun is up and there's no way we're going to sleep in that swelter. I don't know what material they used to make the caravan, but the thing turns into an oven when the sun hits it, and there are way too many mosquitos outside. We chug some strong coffee, then head into the river with our clothes on so we can wash our bodies and garments at the same time. We get out, then strip down to tackle the more difficult chore of cleaning our sneakers. We have to scrub them a long time to get the shit out. Some people stare at us from the bridge: four guys in boxers kneeling on the edge of the Adour River scouring their respective shoes. When we get back to *le camping* in our underwear, wet clothes in hand, we find the campground owner waiting for us. He scolds us in his insufferably amicable tone, though this time we can tell he's fighting the urge to shout. We answer in mono-syllables; neither Ernesto nor I have the energy to speak French. I think we promise to clean the campsite by nightfall. He leaves. Ernesto rolls a joint and says we ought to tidy up a little. Álex objects. 'That clown can get fucked,' he says. They argue. Ernesto claims Paule's honour depends on it, but Álex doesn't care for 'honour' and says that's the dumbest shit he's ever heard. G pulls out his rolling tobacco, and I smoke the second cigarette of my life. Ernesto and Álex raise their voices until they're shouting at each other; an elderly French woman tells them to shut up. We keep forgetting there are people sleeping in the other tents.

In fairness, the campground owner is right. Toss a couple of syringes on the ground, snap a photo, and you could use the image in one of those 'Say no to drugs' pamphlets the state hands out all over Madrid. Our campsite looks like a settlement in Las Barranquillas. We've got into the habit of drinking late into the night (around here any hour after midnight is considered late, even though the heat keeps us from doing much until sundown) and leaving beer cans strewn all over. There are also a few cigarette butts on the ground and the remnants of a campfire we could swear we didn't light. On top of that, our books are scattered all over the site: *La saga/fuga de J. B.*, a volume of Juan Gelman's complete poetry, and *Ender's Game*. We've gone from boredom to despair in the space of a single day, and only now does it cross our minds that pissing on the side of a tree night after night in lieu of walking thirty metres to the bathroom might not have been the brightest idea. Darkness, as we know, magnifies distance. The smell doesn't bother us because our clothes still reek of chicken – damp chicken now – overriding the stink of piss. We hang our clothes up to dry and sit down for another coffee. Too embarrassed to go topless, I decide to throw something on, but the others remain half-dressed. It's 9:30 a.m., the other campers have started to rise and flash us looks of hatred, revulsion, and disbelief. Guess we must be ruining their holidays.

After finishing our coffees, we get dressed and head over to AST. But first Ernesto decides to have a crack at sprucing the place up a little, so we put the books in the caravan, cover the campfire ashes, and take however many beer cans we can hold in our hands to the bins. We have to wait a long time at AST before talking to Élodie. We smoke outside the door and long for sleep. Finally, we go in. We're about to tell her off for not warning us about the gear, but the fat woman beats us to the punch and cites an 'unfavourable report' from the 'employer.' She says she 'can't believe' we showed up to work dressed any old way, putting our own and our colleagues' physical integrity at risk and damaging the company's reputation. This last remark stings Ernesto. I'm sure in his imagination – doubtless inflated by weed – everything we do in this place gets back to the hypothetical Paule. After waiting a few seconds for us to absorb the blow, Élodie adopts a sweeter tone and says 'they' will (who's they?) give us another chance to prove we can rise to the challenge, but we'd better not mess up this time: people with families like Fabrice can't afford to lose hours on account of four bumbling Spaniards. I envy the Cheshire cat's handling of discursive time: her use of a consistently blunt lexicon, combined with slight variations in cadence, softens her rebuke into something like an act of love. Élodie would make a great novelist.

Finally, she asks us to reconvene at AST at six in the evening for another session of *l'attrapage*, this time near the Pyrenees, practically in Spain. We can purchase our gear at a store in the outskirts of Aire. We'll need boots, safety goggles, gloves, coveralls, and headlamps. Ernesto agrees with every word she says, and I don't have the energy to intervene. I fill in Álex and G. G has almost everything we need. Álex raises the point that, depending on the cost, we might not have enough money for the gear. He's right, so I immediately ask the fat woman to pay us for last night's work. Ernesto shoots daggers at me. The fat woman says, 'AST does not pay up front.' I reply that it isn't up front since we already did the work, and she doesn't take kindly to my response. She smiles condescendingly and acquiesces, 'Just this once.' AST will pay us the rest at the end of the month, 'like everyone else.' I bet 'everyone else' gets the same answer.

Élodie rummages in a drawer while Ernesto lectures me in Spanish, saying I pushed too hard and could have got us fired. All I can muster in response is *I wish*. Élodie gives each of us €19.50 and a receipt to sign. We look at her with surprise, even Ernesto. I ask her about the three hours we spent in the car, and she wants to know if sitting in a car counts as work in 'your country.' I glance over at Álex and G, who look like they're moments away from jumping down her throat, then abstain from translating what she said. I tell her those are hours of sleep we won't get back, and she suggests we try sleeping in the car next time, or not taking on night shifts, then adds, 'AST is a serious agency. Turn a job down and we won't call you again. There are a lot of people out there in need of work.'

We leave AST with money in our pockets and the sense that we took a beating, except we don't know why or where the blows came from. It's 12.30 p.m. and we have no clue how to get to the work-wear store. On our way to the car, we pass the Vietnamese restaurant we saw when we first got to Aire. A handful of people are eating inside, and G says we could get something to go in case we don't have time to eat later. We look at the menu and conclude the prices are prohibitive. We decide to eat back at *le camping*, after the shopping trip. We get lost several times.

We reach the shop at a quarter past two. It's a Leroy Merlin–style department store on the side of the highway. Inside is a man who smiles a lot. Everything is insanely expensive. We leave and ask the guy at the garage next door if he knows of any cheaper establishments. 'There are none,' he says. 'It's a monopoly.' The sun and exhaustion fry our brains; thinking has become a task of monumental proportions. The guy says we could always try Pau, though it's an hour's drive and the tolls are steep, meaning it's probably not worth our time. Another option would be to go and see a woman called Marie, who lives in a terraced house about ten minutes from there by car. Apparently, Marie sells things on the down-low to people like us who are trapped in Aire-sur-l'Adour, can't afford to drive to Pau, and need to be at work in four hours (how many of us can there possibly be?). We discuss among ourselves and decide to find Marie.

We get lost again. Either the mechanic's directions were wrong, we didn't follow them properly, or we didn't understand him. We spot a couple of terraced houses and pull over, unsure if we're at the right place. We walk up and down the block yelling the name Marie, pausing at houses 30 and 40 (we think it's one of these, though we've pretty much forgotten what the guy told us). We shout for a while, but no one comes out. By minute fifteen, the rage, heat and exhaustion transform into a kind of hilarious delirium, and we start yelling nonsense, chanting 'U, Pee, and Dee,' crying 'Gora ETA' and 'Visca Euskadi' and 'Marie, Marie! We come for thee!' We get louder and louder. Soon enough, we hear a baby squalling. A young woman sticks her head out the window and warns us in Spanish that she's called the police. Blinds are drawn in another house. Laughing, we ask if she knows a woman by the name Marie, but she just screams at us to clear off and then goes back inside. We leave, surrounded by the sound of our own laughter, the shrieking of cicadas, and the baby's crying.

We get back in the car intending to pick a fight with the mechanic (who probably isn't to blame for anything) but when we get there, he's gone. For the best. It's half past two and knock-off Leroy Merlin is already closing down. It's a miracle they let us in at all. We practically have to beg them to sell us the equipment for a way higher price than its real value. We spend just about our entire monthly budget on farm gear. We don't know what we're going to eat if we run out of food and decide to ration ourselves. G says he has more money than us, given that he only had to buy a headlamp, but we all – including him – know we aren't going to let him share.

In the end, we don't eat. Sadness and anxiety overpower our appetite. I've been writing for an hour and a half; it's six o'clock now. It's time to get ready for *l'attrapage*.

Friday, 12 July
After a ridiculous shift on Monday (a four-hour journey for an hour and a half of paid labour), AST hasn't called us back. The atmosphere at *le camping* is oppressive. We've failed to clear the smell of shit and the neighbours won't stop complaining. We aren't talking to one another. Despite the silence, Álex and G have come to hate Ernesto, who insists on forming a united front with me in a dogfight that I don't understand and am committed to steering clear of. None of us have taken our instruments out save for Alejandro, who plays the harmonica for hours, leading to further complaints from the neighbours and to Ernesto anxiously

smoking one joint after another to cool down. G and I have been reading. None of us will admit to it, but we all want to go back to Spain.

Sunday, 14 July
I read Houellebecq's *The Map and the Territory* from start to finish. An unexpected surprise. It's a social novel where the main character – a guy – takes us through the ins and outs of the artistic field; there is no anecdote outside the field of cultural production (exactly!). The book was recommended by my ex-girlfriend Mónica, now a close friend. Her current boyfriend recommended it to her. I consider ringing her but don't actually want to; besides, it'd be expensive and I'm not sure she's read the book yet. Instead I call Marta, my current girlfriend, and realize I don't have a lot to share. I say things are all right; I have no idea if she can tell it isn't true. My mission to obtain experience, as I referred to it, has been a failure. I have a new understanding of Piglia's famous question: *how to narrate the horror of real events?*

We're running out of food.

Tuesday, 16 July
Yesterday we dropped in on Élodie to complain about the corporate silence to which she is subjecting us, and today they called up Ernesto. He's going to work on something called *les cailles*.

Sunday, 21 July

We wound up working a lot this week, which means we've barely slept. Anything but the horrifying desert of leisure. Today we ate pizza dough without toppings (except for Ernesto, who still has some tins of *le cassoulet*); all the food we bought has run out, even though we'd strained our appetite to the absolute limit of human capacity. We've talked it through and decided to ask our folks for money – apart from G, who doesn't need more and wouldn't have got it anyway – and tomorrow we're doing a grocery run. In the meanwhile, we'll go to a *centre sociale* Álex found and eat their leftover soup and bread. Apparently a *centre sociale* is a state-funded centre for people without resources, or something of the sort.

It's back-breaking work and we always get the night shift (a good thing, ostensibly; the others eye us with envy). We're not arguing any more because the most we can do is wander around like zombies. Also, we can't be bothered. On Thursday I went to a hostel in town and found a French copy of Houellebecq's *Les particules élémentaires*, leaving *Ender's Game* in exchange. I want to see if Houellebecq *stays up to standard*. I didn't pick up the novel again until yesterday, though I understood very little; either my French isn't good enough or I've been too tired.

Last night we worked at a weird complex not far from here. I don't know if it was a hallucination, but in my mind the place looked exactly like the Counter-Strike *cs_assault* map. Twenty of us were on the same shift, and I treated the whole venture like a quest in a videogame. The job involved pushing cages around on a series of carts, filling them with chickens, then loading the carts into a truck. These chickens were different from the ones we were used to, likely another genetic variety: smaller and bitchier. I realize now that I was working like Fabrice, as if I were somewhere else doing some other thing. The more veteran workers have developed a peculiar hatred of the chickens, as if they were to blame for our shitty jobs; they're always shaking the animals around, hitting them and tossing them in the air. At one point G's arms faltered (out of all of us, he's the one suffering most from the lack of food) and dropped one of the cages stacked on the cart. The cage fell on Muhammad, and someone laughed. El Moro didn't think twice before lunging at G, like he'd just been waiting for the opportunity. He held G in a kind of chokehold while pressing his knee into his chest. He looked ready to kill him. Fortunately, Fabrice acted fast and pulled them apart before Muhammad could unload the first punch (or else we'd have had to start a fight none of us wanted to take part in). The rest of the crew was unfazed and went on working like nothing had happened. Even though Álex, Ernesto, and I weren't in the area when the accident took place, Álex and I immediately ran toward G while Ernesto kept his head down (later, at *le camping*, he'd claim not to have seen the fight but I know that isn't true). Muhammad pretended to calm down and stepped away for a moment. A few seconds later I saw a glint near his clothes: he had a pocketknife in his hand and was slouching toward Fabrice and G. I yelled something like 'Stop right there, mother-fucker' in the Algerian dialect of Arabic – the one I speak – and he stared at me wide-eyed, as if checking those words had actually left my mouth. He hesitated for a few seconds, but my shout had put Fabrice and G on alert, so he pocketed the knife and went back to work. Later, at *le camping*, everyone said they'd have beaten the living daylights out of Muhammad if they'd seen the knife. G and Álex applauded my behaviour, but I'm pissed off I had to show my hand and that Muhammad and I have something in common now, in a way, even if it's just a language, even if it's unintended. The four of us talked it over and agreed not to report the event to AST. No one would have believed us anyway.

Monday, 22 July

The strange feeling of wanting it all to be over and also knowing fewer hours of work means less money. Fabrice tracks his time: he takes just long enough to show others he's sufficiently good at his job for them to keep calling him, while also maximizing his profit by clocking out not a minute too soon. He tries to teach us his ways, but we can't help working at full speed; we always want the day to end as soon as possible.

The money made it safely and we bought some more food.

Tuesday, 23 July

Today G and I went to *les canards* (the ducks), far and away the worst gig. You have to use this thing that looks like a gas hose to ram food down the birds' gullets until their livers explode or something, and they stop fighting. Plus, they smell way worse than the others, worse than *les cailles* (some bird I'd never seen before) and worse than the chickens. Everything still reeks in *le camping*, but at least the atmosphere has eased up a little.

In the car G and I talked about the teachers and students of La Autónoma, as well as literature. We didn't mention France. In a way, one car is the same as every other car (ha) and we acted like nothing had happened. It was great; I'd missed talking to G. Then came the ducks.

On the drive back they dropped us in front of AST. As we made our way back to the campground, we half-jokingly wondered if Ernesto and Alejandro had killed each other (we were a bit worried, if I'm honest) but they were fast asleep, Ernesto in the caravan and Álex on the blow-up mattress next to his harmonica. It looks like they've both figured out how to act as if the other person doesn't exist.

If there's no work lined up for us tomorrow, we should probably wash our uniforms, which are piling up in garbage bags next to the tree.

Thursday, 24 July

Nothing since Tuesday. The pressure and boredom are back. We've done the maths and it looks like our wages won't be anything out of this world (we all feel like we've worked way more than we actually have). No one has raised the possibility of going back to Madrid on 1 August.

I have no idea what's going on in *Les Particules élémentaires*.

Our dirty clothes are still by the tree, attracting mosquitos. We'll have to wash them tomorrow, no excuses.

Ernesto caught the Belgian girl and the seventeenish-year-old blond guy from Germany hooking up in the shower. Apparently, they were half-naked. She's been eyeing us with a mix of alarm and fascination ever since.

Monday, 29 July
I've made some money and gone vegan.

We've been here for three weeks, yet the implications of this job only sank in this morning.

In the postmodern age, horror is not a holocaust, but something far more intimate and painstaking. I've reread some of my journal entries and get the sense horror may actually be a metaphor for something else.

They picked me because I've had a driving licence longer than the others. I was about to turn down the gig and send it all to hell when Élodie told me drivers actually get paid for their time on the road, so I said yes (even though it was a day job, i.e., €10 an hour instead of €13; we clocked in at six in the morning, just when the hourly rate was marked down, and clocked out at one in the afternoon). The category was *les poulets* and the subcategory – new to me – *la vaccination*.

In the car I figured out why everyone drives so fast. There were five of us: four strangers and me. None of the guys could come; *la vaccination* is considered a privilege (it's several hours of work in a row) and I was just 'lucky' they'd been short a driver. We were following two other cars. I lost sight of them pretty fast, but Élodie had the sense to stick a man called Michel in my car, and he knew the way. Michel is blond, though his complexion is dark from working in the sun. He has the sort of craggy skin where every wrinkle is visible, which makes him all the more beautiful. He is extremely tall and very strong and broad-shouldered. His head is small, and he has blue eyes.

About five minutes in I understood something fairly obvious: transportation isn't paid by the hour but by the kilometre, so it doesn't make sense to drive at the speed limit, at least not financially. I stepped on the accelerator. Ernesto's mum's car – read: *one of Ernesto's mum's cars* – is a Suzuki Swift, which is light and skids if you speed on the curves. The faster I drove that morning, the better I understood Fabrice and the other guys: the life of an AST worker (I wonder how many ASTs there are in France and the rest of the world) consists of two things: sleeping badly and rounding up frightened animals. All other activities – sex, food, driving, whatever – are secondary. This means that everything needs to last as little as possible, minus work (which will last however long it has to for maximal profit) and sleep (which never lasts long enough). Still – I may as well say it – I wouldn't have minded dying that morning.

It wasn't long before we caught up with the others and overtook them, but then we had to wait a quarter of an hour for them to reach our destination.

Today work has shown me the true nature of animal exploitation. The site reminded me of the end of the world: a massive, modular, bleach-white industrial unit in the middle of a scorched wheat field. In the background the sun rose, wanting to drown the world in the blistering colours of dawn but finding everything in that narrow space to be yellow or white, and nothing else. Access to the complex was through a pavilion-like annexe. We got in a queue, and a veterinarian handed each of us a soft plastic suit that looked like a giant, shiny white potato sack, and a headpiece made of the same material with a see-through window for the eyes. Then he sprayed us with some sort of disinfectant hose. The scene reminded me of Holocaust documentaries, except we weren't so much naked as overdressed. They informed us we wouldn't be able to leave until our (lunch) at break at eleven-thirty. At first I was alarmed because I had to pee, but it took me less than an hour to sweat every last drop of water from my body. Even though I bore it out, I'd go so far as to say it was unbearable.

Sometimes I wonder what journals are for. I have the delusions of a professional author (though this place has knocked me down a peg) and I cannot help but wonder if these words will be published someday. I don't write for me in any case, and I don't write for a particular reader. It pains me to admit that the intended audience of this journal – which is not against the idea of being published in the future – is that nebulous thing people call 'the market,' so I may as well say that the intended audience is you, diary, who have no concept of time and therefore cannot write or be written for a future version of yourself. First off, dear diary, we'll have to figure out the best way to describe the inside of this industrial complex to someone who hasn't seen it before. For starters, we should explain the total absence of smell. One of the main things that sets this job apart from the chicken breeding on other farms is how aseptic it is. To tell the story we want to tell, we would have to begin by locking that someone in a room with ten to fifteen radiators turned on high and then scare them, hang them upside down, maybe even rough them up a bit. Anesthetize them. Push them to the limit. Then we would say: picture a supermarket. (This is one possible approach to the oral portion of our description.) We'd say: picture a supermarket after the end of Western civilization and imagine that the scattered dregs of this civilization live on as sprawling expanses and office blocks. Now imagine that the public servants of this fascist regime or the specimens of the hyperintelligent race that has eliminated the northern half – another thing we'd have to explain is that the north isn't actually a place – of the world have their own ideas about what a supermarket is. The architecture of these supermarkets is the same as that of our supermarkets, except all the shelves in all the aisles – which stretch so far back you can't see the end of them – have been cleaned out and filled with tiny cages you'd never in your life have thought could hold twenty chickens. A couple of veterinarians wander the aisles. They're wearing white coats and masks, and jotting things down. Everything is white, dear diary, brilliantly white – 'Get it?' we'd tell them – white like the end of something, or white like the end of everything. The animals' life cycles are regulated by neon lights that stimulate them to lay eggs and then send them to sleep when they can't take it any more. The only way to tell time in this market of living things – we workers are also part of the merchandise – is by the whistle that goes off at regular intervals (every twenty minutes, I found out later) and is followed by the dumping of large quantities of corn into gutter-like troughs where the chickens go to feed. They are fattened up with light and corn so they will live several days in a day and several lives in a lifetime. You can tell which eggs have been laid by these chickens (Michel told me afterwards) because in France they are stamped with the number three.

My job consists of the following: Michel – doubtless the only person working with me today who is actually nice – has picked me to be his partner (out of pity, I assume). We walk to the end of one of those extremely long aisles. There are seven rows of cages per aisle, a hundred cages per row and twenty laying hens per cage. The last cage in the last row is empty; the goal is to grab a chicken from the second-to-last cage, vaccinate it and then move it to the last cage, the empty one. That way there's always an empty cage available for the transfer – an optimal system that can be repeated ad infinitum. I'm the one who grabs the hens, which, if you ask me, makes this job just another variation on *l'attrapage*. Only these chickens, which are overstimulated and pumped full of hormones, are also consequently more violent, making this gig more challenging than *l'attrapage*; on top of that, it isn't easy reaching all the way to the back of the cage, where the chickens huddle together.

While Michel may be hateful to the hens, he is an angel compared to the rest of the team. You can tell he's done this a lot: I pass him a chicken, and he vaccinates it with surgical precision, then tosses it in the back of the next cage. Sometimes we hear the snapping of a foot or a wing. When this happens, Michel laughs and swears at the bird with a word that gets muffled by the headpiece. I want to hate him but then I look at the other guys – who are far worse – and can't help but hate all of them, who (I suppose) in turn unleash their hatred on the chickens (the cycle ends there: chickens cannot hate). At the start of my shift, I come across the occasional mangled or dead chicken. In the case of the latter, protocol dictates we're to call the vets so they can retrieve the corpse and replace it with a live bird.

It wasn't easy at first, but I'm a fast learner. The right procedure for this variant of *l'attrapage* is to grab the chicken by both wings at the same time; that way your partner can hold it in the same position, turn it round and inject the vaccine in its abdomen. It took me six cages to learn the ropes. On the third cage I broke one of the chicken's wings. I cried. Thankfully the headpiece hid my tears (I don't want Michel to know I am weak). It suddenly dawned on me that some are cut out for this work and some aren't. Then I realized that that wasn't a factual statement but a kind of classism that justified my sense of superiority. I have a degree and will eventually find a job – a precarious one for sure, but definitely better than this one – where I won't have to torture living beings or be tortured for money. If experiencing life in order to write means working as a guard at a *camping* in Barcelona or even as an army nurse, then sign me up. But this is beyond me (maybe the others think they can do it, the way addicts think every addiction is manageable except their own). Still, today I learned that everyone is equipped to do this; by the end of my shift, I was tossing chickens and laughing as maniacally as Michel (thankfully the headpiece takes the edge off the despair).

Eleven-thirty came around and we broke for lunch. We were each given a bottle of water and a cardboard box filled with deep-fried drumsticks. The moment I opened it I knew I would never eat another chicken or egg again (I may yet extend this resolution to milk, yogurt, and all other animal products). Michel, who must weigh about 90 kilos, had no trouble eating my lunch after polishing off his own. Obviously, I didn't mention I found it revolting; I just said I wasn't hungry, that in Spain we have lunch later in the day.

Writing this, I get the sense I haven't done justice to what happened this morning. I told the guys everything in detail and though they were shocked and moved and disgusted on my behalf, they still can't seem to wrap their heads around my resolution to give up meat. They believe it's too radical and that I'll be eating 'normal' food again in less than a week. Clearly this means I haven't explained myself properly. Going off meat – for good – isn't so much a decision as a necessary consequence of this morning's work. There is no other way.

Their response was also informed by something that happened after our lunch break: in a moment of distraction on my part, Michel nearly jabbed my finger with the vaccine syringe. Though he didn't nick me, he was terrified and checked three times to make sure nothing was wrong. At first he apologized, then he got angry and said the injection could have killed me, that I ought to be more careful. Ernesto pointed out that the vaccinated chickens were probably later sold for consumption and he didn't see how we weren't all dead from eating chicken breasts that had been injected with a toxic substance. I think Ernesto was trying to cast doubt on what Michel had said, but the effect of his argument was entirely different: G and Álex reasoned that there was no way that kind of meat wasn't harmful to humans and then Álex swore to go vegetarian as soon as we were back in Spain. I wonder if his vague promise is proof that he was more receptive to my story than the others. I still haven't told them I also plan on giving up eggs, dairy, etc. because I know they'll think I'm crazy. Suddenly, it hits me: twenty-four hours ago, I'd have thought I was crazy too.

There's one problem though: we just went shopping and the fridge is full of meat, cheese, milk, and eggs. I'll have to go on another run soon, except I'm strapped for cash (I picked up smoking and spent what little money I had on tobacco). Thankfully, tomorrow is payday and I made €119 this morning.

Tomorrow I'm going to tell the guys about my other resolution: to quit AST. I have no desire to contribute to the exploitation of animals and humans (*id est:* animals, full stop), to kill myself in the Suzuki Swift, or see Muhammad ever again (he frightens me). So I'm out. I can't handle it. I may not get a novel out of the experience, but I honestly couldn't care less. I know I'm being a coward, dear diary. But it's done. Obviously, I won't ask the guys to go back to Spain with me; I can spend the rest of our time in Aire reading or walking or swimming in the river while they work. But no more chickens or ducks or *cailles*. I wouldn't mind spending the rest of August like this. If need be, I can find another job or ask my mother for money.

The guys are jealous because they heard at AST that *la vaccination* is the best job on account of the seven straight hours of comparably easier work. I hope they get a vaccination shift soon so we can go back to Spain ASAP.

All right, dear diary, you can switch off the radiators and take down our guest. I'm going to hit the shower and rinse away this morning's memories. Then I'll try and get some sleep.

Monday, 29 July (two)

Fabrice was tall and sturdy and always smiling. Not the way the owner of *le camping* and Élodie smile, but in earnest. He was a fast driver and the only person who didn't treat us like we weren't welcome. From him, I learned to mentally check out while my body worked and to grab five chickens at once. We've just been summoned to AST and told Fabrice is dead. Everyone was there. I asked how it happened and all they said was that he left behind a wife and two small kids, and that he'd been a good worker. We held a minute of silence for him, then all went home. Muhammad stared at us the whole time; he looked like he wanted to say something, but in the end didn't. He stayed at AST, chatting with Élodie.

V.
DEATH AND THE COMPASS

I'd like to think that so far any interjections in my original diary have gone unnoticed. I've done my best to respect my past style and have only intruded when strictly necessary or when I thought it might help communicate whatever truth my story may hold.

This morning I went out for tobacco and the ingredients for broccoli burgers. The vegetable shop underneath my apartment was closed so I took a long walk downtown. I saw an unusual shop, a sort of neighbourhood IKEA with mini modular homes on display that immediately reminded me of that journal entry from Monday, 29 July. I think of *les canards'* gullets whenever I fill up my tank, and the server at the bar across the street from where I live looks a lot like Fabrice. I'm not bringing up these connections to elicit pity or sympathy but to convey that my life now is in a way an extension of that journal, such that any and all interjections are as legitimate as the 'original' text.

I think it's time I talked about the Catalans, or rather about the Catalan woman and her appendage, the Catalan man (I can't remember their names). I realize my story betrays certain ideologies I would be ashamed of today. The only reason I've left these betrayals here, making no attempt to hide them, is that I know my past self wouldn't have noticed, as he had yet to come across any criticism denouncing these features of Western thinking. Retaining these blemishes is a testament to the sincerity I promised. That said, it isn't sexism that's driven me to call the Catalan man an appendage or unexpected by-product of the Catalan woman, and it has nothing to do with her being beautiful or us desiring her – she was beautiful, true, though in a ghostly way – but rather it's that she was so rare a specimen, and so perfectly unusual that her strangeness seemed almost like a conscious decision.

From the moment we heard Fabrice had died – actually, from the moment Élodie dodged my questions about the circumstances of his death, or from the moment we realized Muhammad was watching us – we suspected El Moro of being involved in the death of Amigo (we called Fabrice Amigo because it was the only word he could say in Spanish and he repeated it incessantly, and because Fabrice was the closest thing we had to a friend at AST). We wanted to investigate what had happened, or at least speak with Fabrice's wife, but several things got in the way; until we met the Catalans, we were caught up in our own problems, and they confirmed our suspicions.

We came up against three obstacles. First, Élodie informed us we could only be paid if we provided a French bank account number. I know now that she did this to get rid of us and to avoid answering our questions about Fabrice's death, but at the time we were just outraged the way people are outraged by tedious, unwarranted bureaucracy. Apparently, having a French bank account requires one to be French. Luckily, a good friend of my father's, Mustafa – whom I'd known since I was a kid and who was as fond of me as I was of him – lived in Toulouse and agreed to help us out. After convincing the guys that Mustafa could be trusted, I initiated a series of procedures that took about a week and a half. In the meantime, our parents sent some more money to tide us over.

The second obstacle involved *le camping*. Although Élodie seemed happy I'd quit, she decided to punish the rest of the group by not calling them for the following three workdays. I know now that she was trying to get them to leave too, but at the time, Élodie's silence fell over us like the silence of an absent god, and the guys nearly lost their minds. Álex and Ernesto couldn't stand each other. Though G rarely got involved, the few times he did, he took Álex's side. As for me, I watched it all in a daze. Going cold turkey on animal protein had sent me into withdrawal, a condition exacerbated by my total ignorance about anything to do with nutrition, fat, and amino acids (until my mother sent me cash, all I ate was bread, onions, and tomatoes, the only food in our fridge that suited my new diet). I spent the next three days lying in the hammock, pale, chain-smoking cigarettes, totally oblivious to my friends' fighting (according to my journal, I didn't even mind the smell of shit rising up from the mound of clothes beneath the hammock – in the journal entries for the three days following Fabrice's death, I made a single pathetic gesture: shakily scribbling the word *hunger* over and over and over again).

On Thursday, Álex and Ernesto went from words to action, i.e., a fistfight. G watched them stunned and I sat up in the hammock to have a look. I remember wanting to break them up and my muscles refusing to respond; I think I might have had a bit of a temperature, so I just sat there and stared. They rolled around our campsite, then fell on top of the neighbour's tent. The fight ended when Alejandro broke Ernesto's nose; the blood snapped him out of it. A few seconds later the owner of *le camping* was racing at me, screaming. His eyes widened into an expression of horror the moment he saw me (he probably thought I was high), so he immediately turned to G. Ernesto rushed over to intervene and spoke to him with as much sobriety and composure as can be expected from a person covered in mud, wearing ripped clothes and sporting a broken, bloody nose. Álex was virtually unscathed. Seconds after getting up, he was back at the harmonica.

The owner of *le camping* wanted to kick us out straight away. Two things stopped him, one more germane than the other. First, we still owed him a week's rent on the caravan; second, the resident of the collapsed tent took our side (something G and I thought a classic example of

French chauvinism). The owner of *le camping* seized the opportunity to get something out of us: he would let us stay on the condition that we help him nail down the posts of the fence-like structure he was installing around the perimeter of his beloved campground. I remember thinking Alejandro would be put off by this caveat, but in the end it was the exact opposite: he was overcome by the strange urge to work even harder, to the limit of his endurance. In hindsight, I think he'd made peace with the hellishness of that place and resolved to make the most of it, though I never actually asked. Aside from building the fence, we would have to wash our clothes – or rather they would, as I'd already got rid of my uniform – in some sinks we had never noticed before behind the showers.

I mentioned three obstacles. The third one doesn't exactly fit that definition: on day four, I got a job. Besides AST, there was one other temp agency in the area called Adecco, which was about to start harvesting *le maïs*. As much as I'd told myself I was done with work, I knew Alejandro and Ernesto (who had stopped having fistfights and started using their work with *les poulets* as a yardstick for their manliness) would keep us there until August; plus, I figured it could be useful to learn a thing or two about harvesting vegetables, since I'd given up animal products. After double-checking the gig didn't involve chickens or ducks or any other animal forms, I signed up as a *saisonnier* for the corn harvest. The next day, G, who thought he could combine AST and Adecco work, signed up as well.

Ernesto and Alejandro were so absorbed in their paths to self-destruction that they decided to stick it out with AST, even though conditions were significantly worse. They went to the offices several times a day to ask Élodie if she had any work for them, to which she almost invariably smiled and nodded. The more gruelling and distant the job, the more it excited them, and the harder she smiled.

The money arrived on Thursday. From Thursday to Saturday, I walked around and bought food that I thought, intuitively, would contain the basic proteins. I got almost everything wrong but ate enough to start feeling better. G worked the bare minimum. He was waiting until we could start at Synngate – the company where Adecco had placed us – on Monday and didn't want to let go of the AST gig in the meanwhile because *le maïs* – six hours of guaranteed work a day plus extra hours, each paid at €10 an hour – sounded too good to be true. It was around then he started fooling around on his guitar. G clearly had talent, even though he'd only been playing flamenco for a few years, and the Europeans at *le camping* – who'd complained incessantly about Alejandro's harmonica – crowded around to listen. Though G didn't love it, he knew our stay there was hanging by a thread, so he let them watch (although he had a habit of tackling more traditional, inharmonious palos whenever he sensed he was being watched). He claimed to be educating European ears, which made me laugh.

We did an AST gig on Monday morning. I say *we* because I went with them: the guys said the job involved weeding, and no animals, so I asked Élodie to let me tag along. My file was still open and they were short one person, so she said I could go ahead.

It was hands down our easiest gig. We went to a farm about twenty minutes from Aire by car. Álex said he would drive – so he could charge for transportation – which seemed fair. We were greeted by a melancholic, independent farmer on his field. Our task was to check for red spots on the leaves of his corn stalks and tear off the affected ones. It was a walk in the park. We finished the job in forty-five minutes and the farmer said he'd put us down for the full hour if we joined him for a beer. We sat on a hillock that took up most of the cornfield – so small you could see the whole thing at one glance – then drank and shot the breeze. The farmer could tell G and Álex weren't following, so he slowed down and started enunciating a lot. He spoke at length about how badly business was going; by his count, he would be forced to sell his cornfield in less than two years. At one point a helicopter flew over us. The farmer pointed to it and said 'big corporations' sprinkled fungi from light aircrafts and helicopters just like that one, leaving farmers no other choice but to buy their strains, which were resilient but sterile.

Back at the *le camping*, Ernesto and G concluded that the farmer was paranoid. G said 'big corporations' was a generic phrase with no particular referent, a kind of super-structural stand-in for the concept of a vengeful God who scourged humanity with plagues and torrential rainfall.

The farmer, whose magical thinking helped him cope with reality, simply hadn't adapted to new productive models, G thought. I didn't know what to think, so I told them that when I'd gone to the Aire post office to collect the money Mustafa had sent us, one of the clerks had confirmed the bit about the sterile strains. Álex added that he'd watched a documentary produced by an anarchist that corroborated what the farmer had said. In the end we reached a compromise: some agribusiness giant like Monsanto had probably developed a resilient strain of corn that small farmers bought out of convenience, despite it being sterile, but that the stuff about the fungus was just a figment of the farmer's imagination.

Reality and exhaustion had started chipping away at Ernesto and Álex's pride. Ernesto's nose was pretty much healed (and may never have been broken – we didn't take him to see a doctor), meaning the physical reminder of his hatred for Álex would soon disappear. By Saturday afternoon, their relationship wavered between exhaustion and camaraderie, and the four of us went to the bridge to drink beer. Which is how we met the Catalans.

He approached us first. After catching a whiff of Ernesto's joint and hearing us speaking Spanish, he'd come over to ask if we were interested in some weed. He explained that whenever he had an AST gig on the Spanish border, he'd buy an amount for a decent price and then sell it for way less than 'those fucking frogs.' Ernesto had weed to spare but feigned interest so the guy would stick around; the prospect of hanging out with someone from Spain other than us had a palliative effect on him. Ernesto gave the Catalan a toke. The guy then waved at the Catalan woman, who was waiting for his signal at the other end of the bridge and came over to join us. We greeted each other and exchanged names. When he found out we worked at AST, he told us a woman called Marie sold cheap work gear out of a row house about ten minutes from there. We laughed in earnest for the first time in weeks.

We wound up getting drunk at their place. The Catalans lived two blocks from the bridge in a microscopic apartment they shared with a pair of filthy mutts. It was still way better than our caravan. By the front door were two pairs of boots and two laundry bags that reeked of bird shit.

The woman had ginger hair and pale white skin. She said she couldn't take on much work because she was allergic to the sun. The guy was glued to a PlayStation in a corner of the room and started a long string of FIFA matches against Ernesto the moment we walked in. Hours passed and the beer flowed. None of us had eaten, so we got roaring drunk, and the Catalans – who were very reserved – finally opened up to us. They were Barcelona's Jasmine and Aladdin: she the product of a bourgeois family of the *gauche divine* who'd made their fortune with olive oil, and he a gardener at Parc Güell, born in Hospitalet, who'd never met his dad. The story was tediously predictable: they had fallen in love one day while she was strolling through the park with her then-boyfriend. Her family naturally disapproved of their relationship, so they ran away to France; they'd been living in Aire-sur-l'Adour ever since. That was three years ago. She still sent her parents the occasional email or letter, with no return address, but never mentioned her whereabouts. He was thirty-two and she was twenty-five, and they each performed the gender roles that are hammered into all of us as children; though she didn't say it, I got the sense she'd started wondering if it was too late for her to move back to Barcelona, finish her degree in Administration and Business Management, and get a cushy job at her father's company.

Although the part about the Catalan woman's sun allergy was true – this explained her ghostly pallor – it wasn't the only reason – or so they claimed – that they didn't take on a lot of AST gigs. The Catalan woman confessed – with some reluctance from the boyfriend, who left his FIFA match to hover over her and keep tabs on what she said – that when they first got to Aire, they had joined AST thinking something better would come along, like teaching Spanish or Catalan, only to wind up working one seasonal harvest after another (corn, grape, apple, strawberry …). They made some money at first. But then several of their AST colleagues vanished into thin air, with no explanation as to their deaths, and they got scared. Nowadays they only took on the occasional gig, just enough to keep them afloat (her father had kept depositing money in her account, no judgement or questions asked). The Catalan woman seemed on the verge of telling us something else but then only said Adecco was 'a bit better' than AST. That's when her boyfriend politely put an end to our hangout; ten minutes later, we were sitting on the curb. It was half past midnight and the town was deserted.

It was inevitable that we would talk about Fabrice, Amigo. A mix of booze and desperate curiosity led us to make a promise we didn't have the heart to break the day after: to drop in on Fabrice's wife and find out what the deal was with AST. We almost never worked on Sundays, making it the perfect occasion to head over there together. We shook hands, then walked back to *le camping*.

Sunday, 4 August
We went to Amigo's house but didn't speak with his wife.

Facts – I wonder who said this – are always inextricable. Reality is a labyrinth, which is the same as saying it's a desert or a straight line. We can insist that we saw something but never that we understood it.

Ernesto and Alejandro's shift doesn't start until 1.30 a.m. – they left moments before my writing this – so we decided to visit Amigo's wife at 9 p.m.; late enough for dark to have fallen and for no one to see us arrive, but early enough that she wouldn't have put the kids down yet, giving us some time to chat. Amigo's place is in a sort of suburb near Aire, basically a ghost town. The houses are made of particle board and sheet metal; they're like shacks except sturdier (like long-term settlements), and some have been reinforced with brick. There are no lights on in most of the houses. Álex told us the place, which doesn't have a name, reminded him of Comala in *Pedro Páramo*. He's right.

We parked at the edge of the neighbourhood so as not to draw attention to ourselves and walked the rest of the way to Amigo's house. We knew where it was because Ernesto had once dropped off some weed there.

The houses are arranged around imaginary streets and a hypothetical main thoroughfare that doesn't in fact exist. Each house has a garden or the imprint of one: a square of grass around it where nothing has been planted. Amigo's place is one of the best in the area: the ground level is all brick and there is the added luxury of a second floor, this one in sheet metal. If we were to concede that there are such things as street corners in this neighbourhood, then the house sits on a corner. We tiptoed along the left side. Ernesto, who was in front, stopped us with his arm when we reached the end, then pointed to a vehicle that we immediately recognized as Muhammad's red Ford. Next to it was a conspicuous white Porsche Cayenne S.

We stood frozen in place for about fifteen minutes. Inside we could hear a woman talking to Muhammad. Sometimes El Moro shouted and sometimes she did. Ernesto – who has a gift for recognizing faces and voices – whispered that the unfamiliar voice belonged to Amigo's wife. G wanted us to leave, but Álex argued it would be riskier than staying, that they might see us through the window if we moved, and I think he was right. We decided to wait right where we were, quiet and still. After a while, Muhammad left the house with a guy in a suit. They leaned against their cars and lit a couple of cigarettes. The guy was tall, white, and grey-haired. They started talking, but we couldn't hear them. At times Muhammad raised his voice, clearly irate, and yelled things like 'we can't do that to her' or 'they're too young.' Whenever he did this, the other man made a single gesture to shut him up, and Muhammad obeyed. They finished their cigarettes; everything was dark, though their silhouettes were lit by the full moon. The man in the suit handed something we couldn't make out to Muhammad, then got in his Porsche and left. He drove right past us but saw nothing. Muhammad went back inside the house. A few seconds later we heard Amigo's wife yelling *shaitán* and *m'hainek* ('devil' and 'damned' in Arabic) like a mantra, and even though she said little else, the way she yelled those words imbued them with a wide range of expression. El Moro left the house and slowly headed toward his car. Amigo's wife followed him out in a white djellaba and hijab, perfectly visible in the moonlight. She kept cursing Muhammad and gesticulating as if she were giving him the evil eye. Her two children came out with her and stared at El Moro, who calmly lit a cigarette, then got in his car and left. Amigo's family went back inside. The woman cried, hugging her children close to her body.

We waited ten minutes, then went back to *le camping*. On the way there we agreed to stop sticking our noses in where they didn't belong, do the work, and head back to Spain at the end of August.

Alejandro and Ernesto are going to enrol at Adecco first thing tomorrow morning, so we can all start working together.

Monday, 5 August
Today was our first day at Synngate. We didn't work but are getting paid anyway.

We met up with the Adecco people outside the agency, and they took us to some kind of uber-modern facility in the middle of the countryside (i.e., *bumfuck nowhere*). They encouraged us to memorize the route since they weren't going to join us again; as the driver, I am now the only person who knows how to get there. We tailed a red Fiat for thirty-five minutes to our destination and were abandoned in front of a metal gate. The driver of the other car honked the car horn twice by way of farewell. Then we heard a siren and the gate began to open. We drove through it and into the parking lot. There were three other cars there. We laughed on our way into the building. We were in the thrall of an unusual sense of freedom, and not one of us mentioned the previous night's events.

On the elevator ride up we asked ourselves why more people from AST didn't work for Adecco but couldn't think of an answer, or else came up with answers that were either stupid or complacent: none of the other guys were smart enough to go to Adecco and ask, like we had.

We were met by an elegant woman in a suit and a lot of make-up called Hélène. The name *Synngate* was embroidered on her jacket. In fact, it was all over the building, with the exception of the façade. Hélène led us to a small meeting room with an oval table, a projector, and a coffee machine. That's where the rest of the *new recruits* were, as Hélène called them. The new recruits were two girls and a guy. We said hello and Hélène told us we were all very punctual, that the meeting would begin at twenty to ten and that *monsieur le directeur* would be with us soon. She then encouraged us to help ourselves to as much coffee as we wanted and left the room.

Ernesto made conversation with the others. The two girls looked around eighteen, no older than twenty. The guy was in his thirties. Physically, they were exactly what you would expect from the French: blond, lean but strong, tall, a sprinkling of freckles. They appeared to feel very fortunate, as though Synngate were famous throughout France for employing only the cream of the crop – *la crème de la crème*, or whatever. Hélène had taken care to sit all six of us facing the projector screen. Squinting, I saw that the word Synngate was already visible while the rest of the images would remain illegible until the blinds were drawn. I poured myself a cup of black coffee and started reading a pamphlet about the phases of corn growth.

The manager must have walked in without making a sound, as I only registered his presence when G gripped my leg with his hand. I was so taken aback that I failed to suppress an 'ow.' The man was already shaking hands with everyone at the table, starting with the French guy at the far left. I glanced at G, who wore an expression of such sincere terror that the manager – Guillaume – hesitated a few seconds before holding out his hand. Ernesto looked preoccupied as well, though he was better at hiding it. The manager greeted everyone else and then proceeded to talk non-stop about the company, so I didn't get a chance to ask G or Ernesto what was going on with them.

The first part of the talk was a lengthy paean to the virtues of Synngate. Guillaume interspersed his speech with short videos and slides, which meant we were in the dark for a while and gave me a chance to ask G what was on his mind. He replied with a simple, laconic 'Later.'

We learned a few things during those two hours. Founded in Switzerland in 2000 out of a 'deep concern for the environment and public well-being,' Synngate is the result of a merger between Novartis and another company whose name now escapes me. Its origins can be traced to the eighteenth century, and it is the third largest company in seed sales (after Monsanto and another corporation) and the first in phytosanitary products. Alejandro, who was sitting on my right, whispered to me that Guillaume looked a lot like Hank Scorpio in *The Simpsons*, and I couldn't help giggling. I shared this observation with G, though I'm pretty sure he didn't hear me. Alejandro kept calling him by that name, so eventually it stuck.

Later, the guys and I concurred that Mr. Scorpio's video indoctrination had been totally ridiculous and unnecessary. The man remained alert, extremely attentive, and apparently interested in the effect his lecture was having on us. Bent on establishing the extent of our conviction, he passed out a questionnaire (writing 'Synngate is a company with a deep concern for the environment and public well-being' made me feel like I did when I got detention in school or as if I were reciting the Lord's Prayer). The questionnaire had to be completed in French or English, so G and Álex muddled through to the best of their ability. The two girls and the thirty-year-old guy seemed over the moon, virtually ecstatic. They really were delighted to be working for a company like Synngate, with air-conditioned, futuristic offices in the middle of the countryside, suited secretaries, and free coffee. As for me and my friends, if there's one thing that unites us, it's our skepticism, and we didn't get how the French had such an easy time swallowing their propaganda. In any event, it didn't take long for Hank Scorpio to realize that the others had more faith than we did and start giving them preferential treatment. The indoctrination session ended at noon.

From 12 to 2 p.m., Hank Scorpio gave us the ins and outs of the job, showing us his more pragmatic side. The corn we would be handling, he said, was not for human consumption (I bet a good chunk ends up as feed for the region's chickens). He also told us that maize plants are hermaphrodites and that our main responsibility would be to ensure each specimen bred only with itself. According to him, wind action made it possible for them to do this without our involvement, but 'we don't want the varieties to mix, so we implement self-fertilization.' G's reaction surprised me: even though he probably cared less about the environment than the rest of us put together, the nature of our work there horrified him. He found it 'unnatural' and 'atrocious.' Hank also talked about the gear we would use (all provided by Synngate), some safety measures (because it gets very hot, he encouraged us to stay hydrated and take breaks when needed), as well as the nuts and bolts of corn anatomy and reproduction. He also said the maize plants were colour-coded according to when and whether they had been fertilized, a system that functioned on the basis of paper bags. Grey-striped bags didn't mean anything; their only use was to protect the plants' female parts from other varieties of pollen. Once the plants had been fertilized, they were covered with yellow bags, which were swapped for darker-coloured ones (orange, red, brown, black) every day. After black, the bag could be removed altogether as the risk of the plant being fertilized had passed. The bags' design is really handsome.

At two that afternoon, Mr Scorpio informed us we were done for the day, that we ought to get some rest before work tomorrow, our physical and psychological integrity being of great concern to the company. We were to meet at the building complex tomorrow at 8 a.m. so they could shuttle us to the field.

The minute we walked out, I asked G why the sight of Hank Scorpio had shocked him so much. He pretended not to understand the question until after we exited the complex (later he said he'd done this 'in case of surveillance cameras or microphones'). As soon as he felt safe, he asked, 'Didn't he look familiar to you? Hank Scorpio is the guy we saw with Muhammad yesterday at Fabrice's house.' Ernesto had recognized him, but Álex and I weren't so sure, since we hadn't got a good look at him the night before. As we were leaving, Ernesto pointed to a corner of the parking lot, where a white Porsche Cayenne S sat in the shade.

Sure, we entertained the idea of not going back to work, but then Álex convinced everyone that Hank Scorpio hadn't seen us and so we had nothing to worry about. We also decided to stop getting mixed up in the town's goings-on; the plan is to make as much money as we can, then head home to Spain. Even though G wasn't taken with the idea, in the end we all agreed.

The rest of the afternoon at *le camping*, we each kept to ourselves and then had dinner in silence. The guys are asleep. I worry some things were left unsaid.

Tuesday, 6 August
Today was our first real day of work at Synngate. On the way to the building complex and then in the car to the cornfields, Ernesto and Alejandro rehashed some of their worst arguments. G and I sat in the front, chain-smoking in silence.

The croplands weren't easy to access. A small, near-invisible road led to several hectares of cornfields where dozens of teenagers were breaking a sweat. I say *teenagers* because 90 per cent of the people who work for Synngate are circa seventeen or eighteen. They look like they just came from a French summer camp. From the minute we set foot here, everyone has given us the side-eye, as if we were adults intruding upon the happiness of children who aren't ready to face up to the world that awaits them. The only person we had the chance to talk to a bit (until she got angry with G) was Marie, our team leader. If the cornfield is a summer camp, then Marie is a counsellor whose job it is to get along with repeat students (i.e., us).

From an aerial view, Synngate's cornfield resembles a grid city – Buenos Aires, say. There are twenty rows of maize with each stalk corresponding to one city block. An avenue separates one row from the next, and each column is separated from the one before and after by just enough space for one person. Every ten stalks there is another avenue, so that from the sky – several light aircraft flew over us throughout the course of the day – one would see squares of twenty maize by ten.

They split us up. On a regular workday we would each be in charge of one cornrow, but it being our first time, Hank Scorpio asked Marie to assign two of us per row. Ernesto and I are the only ones who speak French, so Marie broke us up, pairing me with G and Álex with Ernesto. A mistake: it took them less than ten minutes to start arguing, and they kept at it all day. Marie watched open-mouthed (then at her wit's end when she realized there'd be no getting them to stop) as they cursed at one another. Today's misunderstanding followed the subsequent script: Ernesto believes Alejandro is an abuser because of something he did to an ex-girlfriend while Alejandro thinks Ernesto is a bougie asshole and prospective Partido Popular voter – he just doesn't know it yet. The two somehow managed to spin a seemingly straightforward topic into countless variations on the same theme.

Things didn't go much more smoothly for me and G, although we didn't bicker (we never bicker). The problem was that G was overcome with the inexplicable urge to rile Marie and refused to stop until he'd succeeded. I was in charge of defoliating the male organs and G of covering the female ones with paper bags, so while he enjoyed a full view of the neighbouring rows, all I saw were his feet. At first he wouldn't shut up about how hot Marie was, which I interpreted as a joke or a sign that he hadn't rubbed one out or got laid in a long time. Then he started shouting what he thought were flirtatious remarks but were actually a smattering of words from his meagre French lexicon. He'd call out *papillon* or *fleur* as compliments, but also *différence* and *pomme de terre*. G had already caught Marie's eye while she filled us in on what to do, and she flirted back to comments she saw as flattery and responded sportingly to what she chose to view as a joke or mistranslation (I guess she didn't want to admit there was a nutcase on her team). The truth is I had a good laugh while G's insanity escalated.

Eventually my partner realized his tactics weren't working, so he started doing everything she had said not to: removing his top, wearing headphones and – a last resort – singing (flamenco) at the top of his lungs. Marie put up with the first two. Ignoring the third would have undermined her authority with the rest of the crew – there are ten of us total, just as there are ten cornrows – so she marched toward us with the intention of censuring G.

I wish I were more like G, but I guess I'll have to settle for being like Munir. G is spontaneous and clever; he is sensitive and fierce. Munir is faint of heart. G is the guy who gets in trouble at summer camp and has a knack for making people think there's a secret reason behind everything he does, one only he can discern. Munir is the guy who winds up having to lie to Marie the camp counsellor for both of them and swearing it won't happen again. Ever since they've known each other Munir has had to make excuses for G – with his parents, partners, teachers, the police, in other words, every authority figure a person might encounter in their lifetime. But Munir laughs a lot with G. He visits him in his holding cell or at the hospital and accompanies him to disciplinary hearings at university; he pretends to everyone that he knows G's secret language when the truth is he's just his friend's condition of possibility, the air beneath the wings of Kant's dove. What happened today is both a caricature and synthesis of our relationship. Marie scolded G for his attitude while I translated.

'*Dis à ton ami qu'il ne peut pas travailler en écoutant de la musique.*' [She wants you to take off your headphones.]

'Tell her to suck my balls.' [*Il a dit qu'il te demande pardon.*]

'*Dis-lui qu'il ne peut pas travailler torse-nu, il va attraper un coup de soleil, et il est totalement interdit de chanter.*' [She says shut up and put on your top or she'll kick us out.]

'C'mon, give me a fucking break. Tell her I know she loves that I don't have a top on. Tell her I can take my pants off too if she wants.' [Smiling: *Il m'a dit que bien sûr. Ça ne se répétera pas, il va éteindre le téléphone portable et il va plus vous déranger.*]

'*C'est bon. Dis-lui que je veux qu'il se rhabille tout de suite.*' [Stop dicking around and put your top back on.]

'Ask her if she wants to have a drink with me tonight at *le camping.*' [*Il dit qu'il a besoin de s'asseoir un moment à l'ombre …*] 'Hey, I didn't say anything about hombres. I asked if she wanted to go out with me. Hey, Marie, *vous voulez* get a drink with me after work? A rum and coke? *Questa nuit?*'

' … '

'Come on, *je sais* you're into me. *Voulez-vous coucher avec moi, ce soir?*'

Laughter rose all over the cornfield, and we learned the true measure of Marie's patience. Neither she nor I knew what to do. For a minute it looked as if she was going to let it slide or maybe even take G up on his invitation. Instead, she let out a series of insults and threats that even made Álex and Ernesto give it a rest. Marie was of the belief that we didn't take the work seriously (she was right) and explained that keeping her job at Synngate was extremely important to her for reasons I couldn't understand (she was yelling a lot and at breakneck speed). In the end she burst into tears, and the counsellor from the adjoining square put her arm around her shoulders and ushered her away. As always, G spiralled from laughter to depression in the blink of an eye. As always, I said nothing.

We weren't fired. Marie came back after a while and begged G to stop. G didn't even bother pretending to listen or understand what she said, but his top was back on and his headphones off, so Marie let it go. I swore G would behave from then on, and she had no choice but to believe me.

We broke for lunch at 12.30 p.m. None of us were hungry that early, so we saved the food for later. I wouldn't have eaten anyway, seeing as the meal was 90 per cent chicken. At first Ernesto and Álex argued, and G looked visibly nervous. Ernesto was threatening to not give Alejandro a ride back to Madrid in the Suzuki Swift, and Álex said he was 'acting like a daddy's boy toward the help.' G was muttering to himself, asking why we were sitting on little benches at a table with a picnic in front of us 'like it's fucking summer camp.' It's true that the situation – working for one of the largest multinational corporations on the planet in such a *naïf* setting, surrounded by minors gleefully eating out of cardboard boxes stamped with the company logo – was unsettling, but G's response was a bit over the top. When he couldn't stand talking to himself any more, he got up and started yelling in trashy Madrileño street slang about how come no one saw what was happening (but what *was* happening?), what kind of fucked-up bullshit were they mixed up in, and why was he surrounded by a bunch of shrimps wearing Synngate pins and Synngate hats doing work that was clearly pointless (and, he said, 'genetically monstrous'), led by counsellors who didn't command an ounce of respect and by Mr. Hank Scorpio, a man by all accounts implicated in the death of an employee of the company responsible for producing the chicken they were eating, which were in turn fed the corn they were harvesting. At first only the kids at the nearby picnic tables fell quiet, but little by little silence spread across the entire open-air cafeteria. Now that I think of it, there's something else that stands out: we couldn't hear a single cicada, not a single insect – nothing at all.

Lucky for us, no one understood a word G said. He ranted and raved until Hank Scorpio came looming through the cornstalks. The minute G saw him, he sat back down in silence, white as a sheet.

Mr. Scorpio was very understanding. He said our friend was exhibiting textbook heatstroke symptoms and it was reckless to work without a head covering. Then he added that what mattered most to Synngate was our health, the health of their employees. He said we looked like clever guys and surely we'd already learned everything we needed to know to begin working at full capacity tomorrow. So, he decreed, the best thing to do would be for us to go 'home' and get some rest. Tomorrow he would personally give each of us a Synngate cap – with visor. The guy smiled the whole time, yet everything he said sounded like a veiled threat (though it's possible it sounded that way to us because we knew who he was).

We drove back in complete silence.

For the rest of the afternoon, G sat on the ground by the caravan, quietly chain-smoking. I tried talking to him about some of the stuff on my mind, e.g., that there was no way we would make it to September without killing one another or at least without Alejandro and Ernesto (who were working at *les poulets* right then) killing each other, but he said nothing.

From five to six in the evening – which is when the heat finally lets up and the French start making dinner and *le camping* comes to life – G threw himself into tuning his guitar and playing a minor chord, 'the strumming of a guitar, like some inconsequential labyrinth, infinitely tangling and untangling,' like the character in Borges's 'The End.' In the centre of *le camping* is a large barbecue grill that's nearly always unlit but that glowed with fire (the campers can rent it for an amount of money unknown to me). For the first time I became aware of the fact that there are alliances, friendships, affections, and resentments (with most of the latter directed at us) in the campground. I also noticed that some of the people who were at the campground when we first arrived were still here now. Little by little, men and women left their tents and gravitated toward the barbecue. The old man whose tent Álex and Ernesto had destroyed in their brawl (aka The Chauvinist) came over to our campsite and explained it was his last day there and he would love it if we came to his leaving do. I translated his invitation. G was keen on the idea, so I said sure, we'd be there. The Chauvinist added that if my friend wanted, they would 'be honoured if he brought his guitar.' G understood the question and surprised me by saying of course he'd bring it (*bien sûr, mon ami*, he beamed). The Chauvinist smiled and walked away from us toward the barbecue.

Before I could ask G what had got into him, he slipped into the caravan and came out wearing a black shirt, his hair slicked back with gel. 'In case the Nympho (the Belgian chick) shows up' was the response he gave to a question I never got around to asking. He grabbed his guitar and walked ahead of me to the centre of *le camping*.

I don't know if G makes me hate him or love him more when he pulls the kind of shit he did today. G brought his *good* guitar with him to France, not his travel guitar. He'd bought the thing from a luthier near the Ópera metro station in Madrid for €450, even though it was actually worth €600 (Antonio Carmona, his flamenco sensei, knew the luthier and got G a discount). I paid for it on the understanding that G would pay me back out of whatever he makes here. I have to admit it sounds amazing, and tonight G played better than ever. He sat on a stump near the fire and started off with a few easy-to-digest palos for all the Europeans. He played alegrías and bulerías, even a rumba. I should have known what was coming the second I heard him playing a rumba, but everyone was so charmed that I let my guard down. When he had everyone's attention – the Nympho's eyes were gleaming and G smiled at her between each song – he gradually shifted toward more jondo or sophisticated palos: malagueña, soleares, and a siguiriya that he didn't so much play as slap out like a psychopath. Before losing the audience, G wrapped up the concert with a saeta ('El Cristo de los gitanos'), which he sang terribly, screaming at the top of his lungs and howling off-key to appalled looks from our neighbours. No one was going to clap, but the Chauvinist lavished him with such enthusiasm – he even had the nerve to tell the rest of the crowd that *that* was how you sang *real* flamenco – everyone gave him a standing ovation. It was the poor old coot's farewell party after all, and G had stopped playing, so why the hell not. I think everyone expected him to stand or give a slight bow or something. Instead, he shut down the applause with a feverish cackle. Then he got up from his seat and yelled that they were all a bunch of morons who didn't understand anything and never would, not ever, then ran to the grill and hurled in his guitar, sending bits of meat, fat, and embers flying into the air. More than a few people raced to their tents – I imagine they must have heard about us and that in their imagination we were nothing short of terrorists. G kept bashing his guitar on the fire like a lunatic. The wife of the campground owner swore at him in French. The old Chauvinist ran in circles like a German shepherd, trying to wrangle the absconders. I pictured him telling them that *that* was *real* flamenco – it always ends with a guitar hurled at a grill – and couldn't help laughing. The campground owner – who seems to think I'm the only sane person in the group but is also a bit suspicious on account of my being part Algerian – shot daggers at me. This is when Álex and Ernesto arrived, trailing behind them an intense reek of shit, which convinced the last few stragglers that the party was indeed over and they should hop back to their tents, caravans, and bungalows. The only people left were us and the owners of *le camping*, who didn't stop swearing at G, not even to breathe. Alejandro, Ernesto, and I eventually carried him off, and I was once again in charge of convincing the owner not to kick us out (it wasn't too hard this time, as we hadn't broken anything; the only thing the man cares about is his property). I picked up the bits and pieces of guitar, which had been reduced to – the biggest part of it, I mean – a small wooden boat with a chunk of mast on the prow. Then I went back to the campsite.

Álex and Ernesto are smoking in silence and G has gone for a walk. So I've started writing on your body, dear diary. On days like this, I can barely stand myself.

VI.
JOURNEY BACK TO
THE SOURCE

I can't work out the secret mechanism by which the death of a guitar managed to unite us the way it did. I won't dwell on what happened the five or six days after that night; it was a happy time and happiness cannot be narrated. That week our work at Synngate was exemplary: the counsellors held us up as role models and Hank Scorpio even implied that if we went on like that we might be promoted to *chefs de groupe*. Back at *le camping*, we tacitly set up a rotation for nailing down the fence, doing the laundry, tidying the campsite, and grocery shopping. I've written *tacitly*, which may require some additional clarification. In her novel *Malas palabras*, Cristina Morales puts forward the idea that love and happiness can only emanate from an assembly-led organization if there is an automatic, intuitive system for decision-making: coming together to wordlessly decree that it will be a sunny day of blue skies is the only way forward. In those days I understood she was right (or more precisely, I revisited my diary after reading her novel and knew she was talking about something like what we experienced back then). For a week no one said anything about who ought to tidy up, do the shopping, work on the fence, or drive. We were a single synchronized body; I doubt we said as little to each other in the course of our relationship as we did then. We only opened our mouths to joke and laugh at things on the other side of the membrane between us and the rest of the world.

On Sunday that zen, *zanshin*, *Dasein*, or whatever-you-want-to-call-it feeling reached its climax. In the morning, Ernesto – who'd acquired a number of survival skills some years earlier – fetched wood from the other side of the river and fashioned a rudimentary bow and a few arrows. We tarred the arrows with some rags, gasoline from a generator near the toilets, and spare car oil from the Suzuki Swift. That night we held a Viking funeral for G's guitar. Ernesto got everything ready: he called over the Catalans, rolled four or five blunts, and led us to the banks of the Adour River where he'd set out everything we would need. We drank and smoked until we couldn't take it any more, and then the funeral started. G had stuffed his guitar with straw and the bits and pieces I'd collected on the evening of the barbecue. He made sure it could float, then rocked it back and forth on the water, placed the six strings inside the funerary boat and released the guitar into the gentle current of the Adour River. We watched it slowly drift away. Once it was far enough, Ernesto picked up his bow, lit an arrow, and released it. He missed by a hair. I tried and also missed. Alejandro hit it full on. The six of us stood there expectantly for the few seconds during which it looked like our plan had failed. Then the guitar was suddenly aglow and we yelled and danced and raised our cans of store-brand beer.

In November of the previous year, Alejandro, G, and I had travelled around Mexico (in search, needless to say, of *experience*). A useful trip in terms of return on investment: we lived in a Zapatista caracol for a month, marched against Peña Nieto on the day he took office, smashed the windows of a Starbucks with rocks, and took peyote in the desert. I wrote a story there ('White Eyes') in which the drug (a wholly imprecise term to designate peyote) isn't mentioned once. We were told we wouldn't find hikuri – that's what the Huichols called peyote – but hikuri would find us, so we spent several days wandering around El Tecolote, a small settlement somewhere in the San Luis Potosí desert. The night hikuri tracked us down, it started pouring. Plus, the drug barely had an effect. We had no idea how to get back, so we spent a freezing night sleeping under the desert rain. That evening Álex remembered that the best way to fight the cold was to lie naked in a sleeping bag, creating a sort of greenhouse effect, so that's what we did: we zipped our sleeping bags together into a kind of super-sleeping bag, crawled inside, and held each other naked. We had the same feeling after the death of the guitar: as if our embrace shielded us from everyone and everything, forming a membrane between us, the world, and its profound disillusionment. Deep down I think we knew something would pull us apart sooner or later. In Mexico it was the sunrise. In Aire-sur-l'Adour we were separated by something much more complex than the rising sun.

Michel was blond, but his complexion was dark from working in the sun. He had the sort of craggy skin where every wrinkle was visible. This didn't so much spoil his looks as make him more beautiful. He was extremely tall and very strong and broad-shouldered. His head was small, and he had blue eyes.

Sunday night after the guitar funeral, Ernesto and Álex were summoned to AST. There was no mention of work; we instantly knew something was wrong. All four of us went there and were informed of Michel's death. This time I didn't ask questions or check if Muhammad was staring at us. We walked back to *le camping* in silence and – though Ernesto and Alejandro wouldn't start up their feud again until the next day – that night we knew something had broken, or broken again.

Monday, 12 August
Ernesto and Alejandro got into another fight. This time G and I didn't step in because hurling reprimands and insults is as good a way as any to not talk about Michel's death. When we got to the Synngate fields, we were given some good news, which sparked a truce between Álex and Ernesto: we'd been chosen to work *les champignons*.

Les champignons is better compensated than *le maïs*; it counts as overtime and pays €15 an hour. Being chosen for *les champignons* entails something else too. The teens view it as the precursor to the role of *chef de group*, which we refer to as *counsellors*. Marie and the teenagers congratulated us, and all morning we were precise and driven in our work, as if to make a point that had in effect already been made. The truth is it doesn't make sense for us to become *chefs de groupe*, since it would mean spending a whole year in Aire, which is something none of us want, as far as I know. But it's a way as good as any to not think about Michel. Plus the overtime, of course.

As usual, *le maïs* ended at four on the dot. Hank Scorpio came over and ushered us into his car – not the Porsche Cayenne, naturally; he drives a pick-up truck with the company logo to the fields. With us were a boy and a girl, both French and a touch older than the average Synngate employee (they were probably around twenty-three or twenty-four, like us). Hank, who gabbed cheerfully on the drive, had made sure Ernesto sat next to him, and Ernesto, who always smoked a joint during every break, provided him with all the conversation his heart desired. Hank had a basic grasp of Spanish, so the two used an off-the-cuff koine that just about allowed them to talk about how beautiful it was there, and hot, as well as the pick-up's fuel consumption.

Twenty minutes later we rolled into the field of *les champignons*. I know now that Scorpio took a long, roundabout way there and back, but at the time I didn't notice or suspect anything. G confessed to us some time ago that the prospect of being in a car with Hank Scorpio petrified him, but when we got to the field *monsieur le directeur* left us in the care of a man in a lab coat and promised to come back for us at six that evening. G was able to relax a bit.

The first thing that surprised us about the field of *les champignons* was the fact that it's a sort of miniature version of *le maïs*: a single twenty-by-ten square of maize with much smaller specimens – about as high as our belly buttons – that are identical to normal plants in every other way. Kind of like maize bonsais.

The whole area was blanketed in a thick fog. The scientist asked us to stick together and hold hands single file. We followed him to a white hut I hadn't noticed before. Inside were lab coats, gloves, safety goggles, and masks in all sizes, and the scientist told us to grab a set each. Then he passed around some cans filled with tiny, colourful spheres that looked like grey, red, blue, and yellow sweets, and did a demonstration of what the job entailed. We were to use small plastic ladles to deposit piles of sweets around the axil, where each blade meets the stalk. And that was it. It sounded pretty straightforward to me, and I was glad there would be no getting on tiptoes, crouching, cutting myself on leaves or overheating.

The scientist smiled and asked if we had any questions. Ernesto said he thought we were there to harvest mushrooms. The man laughed and the French pair looked at us with surprise, as if we'd failed to grasp some obvious piece of information. '*Ce sont les champignons,*' said the scientist, pointing at the cans of sweets, adding that we were to avoid touching them with our bare skin at all costs. Because corn leaves are sharp, all Synngate employees wear shirts with long sleeves and high necklines (despite the sweltering country summers), so it wouldn't be too hard. The scientist taught us to tuck our shirt sleeves into our work gloves and our safety goggles into our masks, then once again insisted that *under no circumstances* were we to let the sweets graze our skin.

Outside the hut we discovered that the combination of fog and safety goggles shrank our field of view to about one square metre. The scientist switched on a bright, red anti-fog light on top of the hut and said that this way we wouldn't get lost; if we became disoriented, we simply had to walk toward the light. Ernesto asked why there was so much fog when the sky above the cornfields had been cloudless, but the scientist pretended not to hear or understand the question.

He set each of us in front of a cornrow, popping in and out as we worked, massive notebook in hand, observing the plants, touching them, jotting things down. He corrected us several times at first, but we're quick studies, and soon enough he was wandering around taking notes. G was in the row next to mine. Every time the scientist drifted away, he'd whisper at me to come close, but the field was small and it never took long for the scientist to circle back. We made slow progress. We had to stick our gloved fingers between each leaf, making sure *les champignons* were lodged in the axil. After about an hour, we heard the hut door open, and G came over to me. He was pale and looked either terrified or repulsed, possibly both. Writing this now, it dawns on me that G is always the first to realize what's going on (note to self: check other journal entries to corroborate this hunch). He pointed at a plant in the row before his – which was unmanned – and told me to go and check it out. Though it took me a while to get over the fear, eventually I glanced back at the hut a couple of times and concluded that if I couldn't see the scientist, then he couldn't see me (I have some doubts now as to the soundness of my logic). I asked G to warn me if he heard anything and walked over to the plant.

My whole life I've got this bad itch whenever I see armies of ants clustered together, or cockroaches, or rotten fruit. I suppose it's natural for humans to fear microscopic things, a fear that in my case manifested as an itch. Sharks and lions are terrifying, but most of us perish at the hands of bacteria or the slow oxidation of our cells. That evening, my age-old fear was reawakened. On the plant G had pointed out to me – and all the other plants in the row – an infection was spreading, making my entire body crawl. Though there was a clear relation between the parasites I was seeing and the sweets in our tins, to this day I still have a hard time believing those blue worms and grey snails were the next growth stage of *les champignons*, which looked more like tiny gummy bears or jellybeans. The red pills had turned into a kind of shiny slug, while the blue tubes were worms, the grey beans snails, and the yellow granules small blemishes that mixed here and there with the green of the plant. The infected specimens were starting to die, but then when I glimpsed the plants in the next row – also infected – they looked much healthier. Needless to say, that small zoo of decomposition was perfectly still, its movement too slow to be perceived by the naked eye. The creatures reminded me of those limpets and mussels you see on the breakwater on one day and have shifted five centimetres over on the next. They were wreaking a slow, inexorable devastation on the plants. I wanted to check out the state of the other rows, but G whistled at me, and I saw the scientist walking toward us. I had just enough time to slip a fistful of sweets into my shirt pocket, though not to get back in position before he saw me.

The scientist asked what I was doing outside my row. The answer I gave was both difficult to believe and imposs-ible to refute: I'd become disoriented in the fog and started walking along the column instead of the row, vertical instead of horizontal. Without realizing it, I had given the perfect response. If the scientist decided I wasn't telling the truth, then I'd seen something that merited lying to cover it up; on the other hand, if I really had got confused and started working the columns, I could have ruined months of progress in a matter of minutes. A look of painful indecision, one of utter, childish denseness, flitted across his face. Then he yelled loud enough for everyone to hear him – *arrêtez!* – and said we were done for the day, we could stop working. It was 5.30 p.m. and the French boy protested: he'd been told we would be paid for two hours of work. In response, the scientist took off his gloves, grabbed his cellphone, and rang Hank Scorpio to come and collect us. Then he walked everyone to his lab to return the equipment; on the way, I saw G dropping small fistfuls of *champignons* behind him.

If Hank Scorpio was worried, angry, or nervous, he did a good job of hiding it. He made small talk while taking the same long, roundabout route to *le maïs* (we had to pick up our car) – it was more obvious to me this time, even though I wouldn't have been able to find my way back. Back at the car we were surprised to find that there wasn't a single sign of fog.

We talked on the drive to *le camping*. The four of us saw eye to eye on the facts: we were being paid 150 per cent the usual rate to infect bonsai corn. But our interpretations differed. While Alejandro and I were more radical in our view of Synngate's capacity for evil, Ernesto believed in a free-market trend toward environmental balance, and the only thing G knew was that he felt a white-hot rage and primordial disgust toward Synngate, AST, and Aire-sur-l'Adour. At some point in the conversation Ernesto jeeringly asked if I was going to stop eating plants too and subsist only on water and sunlight. Although his observation was valid, his tone annoyed me. Plus, we were all a bit high-strung, and he and I wound up screaming at each other in the car. On the surface our argument was about veganism, but it was actually about something much deeper that I can't seem to put into words. A period of silence followed. Then, as we were entering Aire, Ernesto told us he'd learned a couple of things from talking to the French pair.

First, he said, the least important: the fat woman at AST is Hank Scorpio's daughter. Second, the most essential: Synngate employees are as young as they are because, all joking aside, *le maïs* is a summer camp for students from a school for French Navy orphans. They send them there in the summer to work and save up for university (orphan benefits – Ernesto says they told him – aren't very generous in France and the extra money is a boon). Some of the kids work there after finishing high school as well (for example, Marie and the other counsellors). The four of us are little more than a coincidence or glitch in the system: there comes a time every summer when Synngate needs more muscle to meet their deadlines, so they ask Adecco to send them a few people. Neither detail is especially horrifying (though Élodie being Hank's daughter is a little troubling), yet for some reason it was more than we could handle emotionally, and G and I started crying like babies.

We've decided to go out tonight and see what's cooking in Aire. I showered first, then started writing on your body, dear diary, while the others washed and got ready. We're in our Sunday best, G and I are on our fourth beers, and the night is glorious, like all summer nights in Aire, where it smells of jasmine and the river makes the air feel pleasantly cool, so we're going out, dear diary, and tomorrow's another day.

VII.
SLAUGHTERHOUSE-FIVE

The story of the four men we used to be – or so it's said – is coming to an end. I'm not going to reread what I've written or transcribed, though I imagine there are readers out there who feel the rhythm, tone, and style of this text aren't exactly apposite (for what? for whom?). Unfortunately, reality – unlike a life story – doesn't have to conform to the narrative demands of readers. In a sense more commonplace than historical, Lenin was right: 'There are decades where nothing happens; and there are weeks where decades happen.'

Anyone who entrusts their life story to a journal knows the imprint of the world is a necessary condition for the journal to exist. In reality – though this is something known only to those of us for whom journals are a central vice – the journal is the condition of the imprint and not the other way around. For every piece of writing, there is an outside that slips through the slats; the diary is the genre where this outside is more present.

In journals, the exterior operates in unsuspected ways. The most evident of these is a riff on the cliché that claims journals narrate raw material, i.e., life. Life, then, would determine the content of the journal ('the price of electricity went up') and that interjection is potentially severe ('The price of electricity went up. The situation has become untenable. Laura and I have decided to leave the country, though we don't know where we'll go.'). But believing the relationship between journals and life is as simple as this betrays a level of innocence I do not possess. A more sincere intervention, more involuntary and more subtle – the second degree of this exterior incursion, to give it a name – occurs in the dense thicket of the unsaid, which is a nexus between the reality inscribed in the journal, the inscriber, the narrator – a phenomenon that arises from the inscription itself – and the reader. When we read that 'the electricity went up,' we don't picture a bolt of lightning or a watchman climbing the mast of a sailboat with a flashlight between his teeth; we picture an exploitative bill, a little thing called power companies, a system that encroaches on our bodies, pushing them to work to the limit, etc.

The most fascinating kind of real-world interference happens when the event itself is removed, and all that's left is its impression. Imagine we find two volumes of a journal with the same handwriting. The first tells a political tale, rife with militancy and conflict, and stops mid-story. The second is the trivial account of one person's day-to-day routine; it also stops abruptly, but nearer the end. We sense the traces of a war, an ascent to power, the imposition of a fascist, hypervigilant regime, and the eventual disappearance of the person writing the journal. Maybe the authorities had come across the first volume, or some letters, or maybe the writer was just in the wrong place at the wrong time. It doesn't matter. The moment we sense these traces, we read his routine in another light; maybe every time a bakery is mentioned it means something else, that he was meeting a contact or delivering a package, a detail that was nonetheless silenced, a feature of the outside world trying to force its way inside.

This type of incursion doesn't only take place in the content of the journal but also in its form and chronology. Maybe Laura and the writer of the journal emigrated, and their voyage was never recorded. Maybe there followed a handful of well-spaced notes, with entire weeks between one entry and the next, many of them cut short. Then the rhythm changes: some days are flooded with page after page of awestruck descriptions of New York City, though each entry is written with a different pen (at every boarding house and every inn, they borrow a new writing utensil). The ever-dwindling references to restaurants and cafés speak of money problems that are never directly addressed. Finally, the entries grow shorter and shed their rookie excitement. With nothing to say about his own life, the writer starts discussing the books he's read. This is followed by fleeting, often desperate literary reflections, then silence. The man has found a job and slowly neglects the journal, its entries thinning out until none are left, just blank page after blank page; the journal becomes a kind of monument.

A practical example: a journal entry from a few days after we worked *les champignons*, which on the surface has nothing to do with France, corn, or Synngate, yet still reflects obsessively on all of the above.

'We in the West are incapable of conceiving of intelligence without ambition. Capitalism has taught us that intelligence as a trait increases production and output, improving time management and eliminating all the nooks and crannies in which fiction can be made. The intelligence of maize plants that reproduce according to fractal logic, or of a flock of birds flying in perfect geometric formation, does not, to our minds, constitute true intelligence. Neither is an elderly mother intelligent, or a painter, or a medieval engineer who polishes a rock with only his intuition [Deleuze & Guattari]. We can picture this engineer polishing the arches of a Gothic cathedral more successfully than any other guild member. Yet we know it's the other man's technique that will prevail, because it is systematic and repeatable; the intelligence of our engineer refuses to be tied down, it wants and needs to nurture the nooks and crannies of his knowledge of the rock.

'Another example is that of a gymnast who knows every muscle in their body or of a musician who barely understands what they are composing. The musician is intuitive, capable of detecting and producing distant symmetries that are dozens of measures away from each other. They see beauty in seemingly horrid dissonances. Their curse is being unable to share this knowledge, that there is no system behind their understanding of music; no one else can do what they do and hardly anyone understands their work, which is nonetheless as solid as a Gothic cathedral.'

Telling the truth, then, doesn't mean exhausting reality (which is infinite) but laying down its reading conditions, those of the outside world, and weaving together all the unsaid things that make a journal tick.

I can't put off the dénouement any longer, so I'll pick up our story on the day after *les champignons*.

The next morning, I rolled out of bed before everyone else, hoping to get ahead of an apology I knew would have to be made. The evening before we'd got plastered and caused serious damages to *le camping*. No doubt the worst part was when G, who couldn't drive, climbed into Ernesto's mom's Suzuki Swift and skidded around *le camping*, horn blaring. I was riding shotgun and couldn't stop laughing.

The cold light of day revealed the consequences of our actions: we'd driven over the side of a tent and destroyed the swing set. On top of that, there was glass all over the campsite abutting our own, and someone – to this day I have no idea who, since no one owned up to it or remembered doing it – had taken a shit smack in the middle of the Belgian family's campsite.

I made my way to the booth, certain the owners were going to kick us out on the spot. They didn't. It must have been six in the morning, the sun was just rising, and both husband and wife showed signs of not having slept; I assume they hadn't tried to stop us out of fear of what we might do to them in our state. It was obvious they'd come to some sort of agreement, as that was the only time we had a two-sided argument (them-me) that didn't also involve an internal spousal discussion (her-him-me). They'd decided not to kick us out on the condition that we restore any damages caused before the other campers left their tents. They would stay in the booth until we gave them the go-ahead; they didn't want to see what we'd done. I clung to the thought that we were off the hook and put up with all kinds of threats and racist slurs. They also told me we had to pay what we owed (practically all of August) by week's end, including the days left until September. I said yes to everything, then went and told the guys what I had signed us up for.

Ernesto and Álex accepted the owners' terms. G couldn't string together a single word, so we started tidying. We did a fair job of cleaning up and fixing the tents (most of them just had bent or loose poles); the one thing we couldn't properly repair was the playground (which was no longer usable, seeing as the trampoline was now riddled with holes), though it looked great, aesthetically speaking. We also couldn't clear the tracks the Suzuki Swift had left all over *le camping* or restore the slumber the other residents had lost. I think I already mentioned that the heat made it impossible to sleep after 9 a.m., so we had no choice but to suffer their hateful looks while we got ready for work.

That day at Synngate we toiled like zombies under the sun, and G even puked in the plants. But we survived.

Things were a lot quieter the following week. G, Alejandro, Ernesto, and I dedicated ourselves to sabotaging the maize crops, lopping off the stalks in the neighbouring row and mixing different varieties of pollen in the paper bags. Even though Marie and Hank could tell something was up, they had barely any proof, so they got the whole crew together to lecture us about annual yields and crop destruction. But by then all the teens could think about was September being round the corner, which meant they got to go back to Navy orphan school, while all we could think about was how – against all odds – our time there was coming to an end. So Hank and Marie's threats and rebukes had no effect whatsoever. Needless to say, the guys and I weren't called back to *les champignons*, though this didn't deter us. As 1 September drew closer, we became more and more daring, and our sabotage of Synngate more and more destructive.

Clausewitz claims that the best and most enduring way to unite human beings is to create a common enemy. In *Watchmen*, Alan Moore posits the existence of a superior form of intelligence that is watching us and decides the only way to end war on Earth (the book is a bit more modest than that; they'd have been happy just to end the Cold War, which is a metaphor all the same) is to make up an extra-terrestrial enemy against which all humans can band together. That week Synngate, which isn't human, was our alien. These days I get the sense I could use my journal to compile a list of factors that would make a group of people join forces – shame, fear, a common enemy, xenophobia. Or maybe I'm wrong, maybe deep inside each one of these things lurks something dark and unknowable whose own indeterminacy binds them into a cohesive force.

Between Tuesday and Thursday nothing happened. On Friday we did the maths and realized we were broke, then asked Adecco to transfer what they owed us for that month. They didn't put up a fight. Rereading my diary, I remember there was something else that happened around that time: I had a terrible allergic reaction. I'm allergic to grass pollen and until that first episode, I had no idea corn was a member of the grass family. From then on, every cut or speck of dust that drifted into my mouth or eyes led to swelling and unspeakable pain. One day Hank Scorpio took one look at my red eyes and puffy face and threatened to send me to the company doctor, but I refused. Once again self-destruction became a way of resisting an enemy I knew to be undefeatable.

In a novel or short story my allergic reaction would have stood as a symbol for something else. I'd been allergic to grass since I was little, so why had nothing happened on my first day at Synngate? Were a reader to try and pin down some sense in this text, they might conclude that as an author I am saying the horror of that experience overwhelmed my intellectual faculties and manifested in my body. Somatic powerlessness against evil as its best form of identification. But that's not the case. As I've said before, there is no metaphor in these pages, nor any intention. I'm not your average narrator; I don't arrange things or order them, I reveal myself. I don't create characters, I transcribe people (the four of us) and shadows, which is how we tend to view other people; I simply am, like the first *aoidos*, the vehicle of a thing that transcends me (the gods in the case of the *aoidos*, experience in mine), a necessary vehicle for language to be able to tell what really happened.

The following Monday (19 August), facts once again bucked the logic of fiction and hastened (hastening us with them) toward the void. We'd promised the campground owner to pay the agreed amount (everything we owed plus what was left until September) on that day, so we stopped at the bank for our Adecco wages before heading to work.

Things at Synngate went smoothly. As we drove back in the Suzuki Swift, I noticed G seemed agitated. He started telling us an unlikely story about a guy who worked at a shop and was sent to prison by mistake: one day his bosses told him the count in the register was short. He claimed not to know anything. A few days later he discovered he had taken the money home by accident and became irrationally anxious. He wasn't sure whether to return the money, afraid his bosses would think he was only doing so because they had brought it up. We never found out what happened between that and him going to prison because out of nowhere G started talking about Élodie. He applied the iceberg theory in a new, fascinating way, shifting from Story A to Story B with no regard for resolution or continuity. Yet, G's jitteriness and mad gestures made it clear that Story B was implied in Story A.

When a story is well told we don't retain the events so much as the sensations they evoke. Though I don't know what he said, I do know that G managed to make Álex, Ernesto, and me furious, to get something to grow in us little by little, until bursting point, something like driving the Suzuki Swift all over the campground, setting fire to AST, and bombing the Synngate fields. I wish I could share what he said, but a number of things prevented Munir (or 'me,' depending on the convention) from writing in his journal until two or three days later, by which point he had forgotten his friend's exact words. G went on about El Moro and Élodie, about Michel and Fabrice and his kids, about Marie and Hank Scorpio. He said we weren't leaving – *we*, he said, either knowing or assuming he was implicating us the moment he made his speech – Aire until we got to the bottom of the issue of the dead employees, the relationship between AST and Synngate (between Hank Scorpio and his daughter Élodie) and the orphaned workers; that none of it made sense but we had to make it make sense, that we had to make the facts tell Story B.

We rolled into Aire making bald declarations that most people would have agreed with but that nonetheless made us happy, because we were all on the same page. We'd say something like, 'It's a crime they don't pay for transportation to the sites,' then applaud and sit up in the car, patting each other on the arms and shoulders. We'd say, 'Le camping is full of bougie dipshits who hate us but need us at the same time, or else they wouldn't get to eat their precious chicken, eggs, or pâté,' then roar with laughter. We made the decision to plant ourselves in front of Élodie and demand an explanation. We were confident in our heroism, and I sped down the roads, skidding on every curve.

In the second roundabout into town, I hit a boy of around seventeen.

Ernesto instantly recognized him: his name was Abdelkader, and he was Muhammad's younger brother. When we pulled him into the car he was still conscious and told us in broken French that he was fine, then begged us not to take him to the hospital under any circumstances. He looked terrified. In Arabic, I asked why he didn't want to go to the hospital, and he stared at me with a mix of joy and surprise, only to immediately pass out. He was breathing normally and looked as though he was sleeping; there were no visible wounds. We figured he was probably unconscious from shock more than the blow itself, and decided to take him to le camping to drink water and get some rest.

When we arrived at le camping the barrier didn't open as usual. The owner came out and demanded payment if we wanted to be let in. I explained we had an injured boy in the car, and he glanced into the booth – where his wife stood watching – and said no, the money first, then he would let us through. So I collected the cash from everyone and paid him. The moment the bills hit his hands he ran to the booth and locked it from the inside. I stood frozen in place at the barrier with no idea what was happening. Álex pointed at a grey mass that we hadn't seen when we arrived: our effects covered in a large tarp. The tarp was ours as well, and it being there meant they had gone through our things. We uncovered the mound and saw that Álex's cajón was broken and the back compartment of Ernesto's camera empty. We debated whether to call the cops, but Abdelkader was waking up, plus we knew the local police were in cahoots with the campground owners. Besides, it wouldn't have been easy to explain why a beaten-up Moroccan youth was lying in the back of our car. We didn't have to exchange a word to conclude it was time to swallow our pride and get packing. We started shoving things in the trunk under the watchful eyes of all *le camping*'s residents. We gathered our things in silence, deflated the air mattress, separated the perishables from the non-perishables, and stacked our books, until a British guy who lived in one of the bungalows with his wife and two kids remarked – his words crisp in the presiding silence – 'They've taken things surprisingly well. I've always thought Spaniards were on the aggressive side.' Hearing this, my temples throbbed and I was filled with a wrath that had nothing to do with patriotism. I was ready to lose it, and that man had given me an excuse and a target. G acted before I even had the chance to look up:

he grabbed a bottle of beer from the glass disposal bin next to us and lobbed it at the Brit. Everyone at *le camping* started hurling threats and insults. The residents called us beasts, animals, brutes, savages, and a bunch of other things we couldn't make out, in all the languages of Europe. Not even Ernesto could help himself: every one of us furiously heaved bottles at the peanut gallery. I remember thinking we were waging a medieval war and that we held the best position, dominating the battlefield from high ground. Many of the Europeans fled. Ernesto saw one of the campground owners, the wife, pick up the phone to call the cops. It all happened in the blink of an eye: two leaps and he was at the fuse box beside the entrance switching off the power in one fell swoop. The owners got up and opened the booth door, but Álex deterred them with a bottle that plummeted right at their feet. The glass disposal bin and the ground around it were littered with bottles, so we had enough ammo to last a while. The only person left on the esplanade was the Brit, who swept the ground for rocks to throw back at us and missed every time. We kept at it until Ernesto sent a one-litre bottle of beer crashing into the booth window. That's when we knew it was time to retreat. We quickly collected everything that wasn't in the car yet and left before the police could get there. At this point Abdelkader was already lucid and cheering on our bottle war, though he was clearly anxious. That was our last moment of true joy in Aire-sur-l'Adour.

Ernesto remembered the Catalans had a garage and figured they might be willing to give us somewhere to lie low. He was right: their neighbours used it for storage and all we had to do was push a few pieces of furniture aside to fit in the Suzuki Swift.

We called Muhammad El Moro. He was dark-skinned, dark-haired, and terribly thin, too gaunt and bony for his age. He was from Fez. He had black, sunken eyes that looked straight through you, and a hooked Arab nose. He spoke very little and knew – or perhaps couldn't help it – how to make people cower in his presence. His lips were thin, and a scar yarned his mouth, where most of his teeth were missing. That night Abdelkader informed us Muhammad had died.

Reality always fails writers, and back then three out of the four of us thought ourselves writers. There was always Story B, even though it turned out to be nothing like any of the versions we could have come up with. Throughout the past week, on our drives in the Suzuki Swift and during downtime at *le camping*, we'd hashed out several conspiracies, discussed the relationship between the antibiotic shots, *les champignons*, the genetically modified maize, and the high incidence of cancer in the West, offered incest and rape as explanations for the family ties between Hank Scorpio and Élodie, and concluded that everyone who found out about the link between the chickens and the corn was wished away with Muhammad's help; in short, we had invented a Story B that wound up as a cover for

Story C, which is the real story, the story Abdelkader told us and that I translated for my friends and for the Catalans and turned out to be far less surprising but also infinitely worse, because horror is a soft, sticky thing – never effusive, never a bang. There was no mystery, no case, and therefore no novel.

Abdelkader's story was shot through with interruptions. At first he cried at every mention of Muhammad and threw himself on the floor at the sound of police sirens; we turned off the lights so he would feel safe. There was no doubt in our minds that we were being searched for on account of our destructive behaviour at *le camping*, but local police are consistently lazy; and besides, we doubted the campground owner (the only person who had our contact details) would have turned us in, reluctant to air what had happened with the camera, the eviction, the cajón, and the money he stole from us. They only circled the block twice and then probably got bored and went out for coffee or to bed or whatever it is local police do in remote towns in the French countryside. What I mean is that the story was neither linear nor straightforward. It was also translated by a guy who lacked fluency in dialectical Arabic – let alone Moroccan – and was interrupted by sirens and questions from his friends, who at first wanted to square Abdelkader's story with our Story B and then needed to come to terms with the fact that we had got nearly everything wrong. I will summarize everything Abdelkader told us that evening, redacting the hesitation, fear, and crying from his account, not to mention the misunderstandings. I will also redact the breaks, the weed, and coffee that flowed all night long, the uncomfortable questions and suspicions. The story, as I remember it, flattened by time and by that sad skepticism we in the West call 'maturity,' is as follows.

No one had murdered Michel or Fabrice. They had crashed their cars while driving to work. We'd heard that the licenced employees who earned Élodie's trust tended to be given the best assignments: shuttling material from one place to another. Like any trip, AST paid per kilometre travelled and the employees took each kilometre at two or three times the legal speed limit. Owing to the heat, or to the illicit nature of the material transported, the gigs always took place at night, with no advance warning, so it wasn't uncommon for drivers to be called up while drinking at some bar in town or at home on their own in front of the TV. Abdelkader said that the Aire police force was being paid not to fine AST employees who went over the speed limit and his brother was in charge of the kickbacks, even when the assignments' nocturnal nature made the improbable appearance of the national police force – *la gendarmerie* – all the more improbable. What we had were exhausted workers who were not infrequently drunk – and always underpaid – flying through the night on pitted highways, all of which made their deaths a regular occurrence (on this point, the Catalans agreed with Abdelkader). Muhammad's side gig for AST was negotiating under-the-table compensation packages with the affected families, in other words, compensation that the French government would never hear about and was therefore granted on top of any orphan and widows' pensions the victims may already be getting. That way AST didn't have to field awkward questions about their late-night assignments. Hank Scorpio (manager of Synngate and nominal owner of AST) was one of the parties; he was responsible for ensuring the company didn't pay one *centime* more than what it believed the family – whose story was likely to be ignored by the government and the media – deserved. But it's always best – Abdelkader said, perhaps parroting his brother – not to let shit hit the fan. Muhammad received a tantalizing cut of every compensation he negotiated and also became an esteemed member of Aire-sur-l'Adour's community of workers.

The system functioned smoothly until Fabrice died. Abdelkader said Muhammad was especially worried about that case because he was convinced we were following him. He said Muhammad started smoking more weed than usual, which made him even more paranoid. He was right to think we had our suspicions, but the moment he caught us sniffing around and asking questions, his imagination eclipsed our actual intellect to such a point that he never found out just how off the mark we were. Unease and insomnia made him a bad negotiator and Fabrice's family received much less compensation than he thought was fair for a woman who spoke virtually no French and her two small children. We asked Abdelkader for a figure, but he wasn't clear on the details. That must be why Muhammad and Hank Scorpio were arguing that night outside Fabrice's house: over the family's compensation. Muhammad went through a rough patch after that, swapping weed for harder substances, getting drunk every day, blaming himself and us for the deal Fabrice's family got, even for Amigo's death on the highway. Then Michel died and El Moro negotiated with Hank Scorpio like a man with nothing to lose. Mr Scorpio even threatened to fire him from the company and find another negotiator. In the end Muhammad managed to get Michel's family reasonable compensation, but he was never the same again. He thought he was being followed, lost weight, sent Abdelkader to pay off the police, and only left the house when strictly necessary.

The day we ran over his brother, Muhammad was found dead near a poultry farm not far from Aire. All that was left of his car were four wheels and a frame. The case was cut and dried: the car had burned with Muhammad's body inside it. Given their history, Abdelkader suspected Hank Scorpio of killing him. He heard about his brother's death from an AST employee, who called the house to tell him. While on the phone, he gazed through the window and saw the Porsche Cayenne S pull into the street where he lived. He panicked, ran out the back door, and didn't stop running until he was outside Aire. Apparently, he and his brother didn't live far from the Catalans. We hit him with the Suzuki Swift on his way out of town.

As far as you, dear readers, are concerned, this is where our story ends. As for the four of us: Synngate, AST, and

Aire-sur-l'Adour stretch out like a soft, delicate thing into both the future and the past. In a famous piece by Borges, he asserts that Kafka not only changed the face of the literature to come but also of the literature before him. Likewise, our stay in Aire changed not only our future (in obvious ways like my going vegan and Alejandro becoming a journalist) but also our past. There are no morals to real-life stories. Yet, if this story were to have one, it would go something like this: true horror does not know vitriol, only monotony and routine. I imagine the same applies to true happiness, except the other way round: making every minor detail shine, always operating on the microscopic level. For me that experience suffused everything with the smell of chicken and duck shit and turned every act into one described in a lost excerpt of a journal I never wrote. Some people view storytelling as a kind of therapy or a way of getting things off your chest. But that's not true: at most, storytelling – I realize now that G was right – is something we do by instinct while the world falls to pieces around us.

We spent two days in the Catalans' lair. They were supportive at first, though it took them less than twenty-four hours to begin requesting payment for our stay. After hearing Abdelkader's story, they had decided to get as far from Aire as they could (I assume she planned on heading back to Barcelona) and claimed to need money for the trip and other random excuses no one asked them for. We said we understood and would give them some cash as soon as

Adecco paid us. We checked our accounts repeatedly on the Catalan woman's computer, like we were expecting something. The next day the couple went to the supermarket and we grabbed our stuff and left without saying anything to Abdelkader. We never heard another word about them again.

We weren't stopped at the border. Adecco called several times (I imagine they wanted to know why we'd stopped working *le maïs*) but we didn't pick up. Ernesto didn't want to go straight back to Madrid, alleging he needed some time to think, and asked to be dropped off at a majestic old house outside Santander belonging to his family. We spent the night there and, as far as I can remember, barely talked. Alejandro, G and I were silent on the drive back to Madrid. Around Palencia I instinctively took my hand to my chest and found the clutch of *champignons* in my shirt pocket. Some had transformed in the humidity and adhered to the fabric but most were still in a larval state. I chucked them out the window with my bare hands. A few months later the shirt was still covered in yellow stains, and I had to get rid of it.

Almost a year passed during which G, Alejandro, Ernesto and I only rang one another or spoke when strictly necessary, to request a piece of information or phone number. Things between us went back to normal – or what we considered normal – later. We never talked about what happened in Aire-sur-l'Adour. That's not quite right. One day Alejandro asked us to meet him in a park in Vallekas and made us swear to go back to *le camping* to smash the booth window and wreak some more havoc, maybe even set the whole place on fire. To this day we haven't kept our promise, and the subject was never brought up again.

Munir Hachemi's career as a writer began with him selling his stories in the form of fanzines in the bars of the Lavapiés neighbourhood of Madrid. He is the author of *Living Things* (2018) and *El árbol viene* (*The Coming of the Tree*) (2023), and is also a translator from Chinese and English. In 2021, he appeared on Granta's Best of Young Spanish Novelists list. He currently lives in Buenos Aires.

Julia Sanches is a literary translator working from Portuguese, Spanish, and Catalan. Recent translations include *Boulder* by Eva Baltasar, shortlisted for the International Booker Prize 2023, and *Undiscovered* by Gabriela Wiener, longlisted for the same prize in 2024. Born in Brazil, she currently resides in the United States.

Typeset in Arno and Flood.

Printed at the Coach House on bpNichol Lane in Toronto, Ontario, on Zephyr Antique Laid paper, which was manufactured, acid-free, in Saint-Jérôme, Quebec, from second-growth forests. This book was printed with vegetable-based ink on a 1973 Heidelberg KORD offset litho press. Its pages were folded on a Baumfolder, gathered by hand, bound on a Sulby Auto-Minabinda, and trimmed on a Polar single-knife cutter.

Coach House is on the traditional territory of many nations, including the Mississaugas of the Credit, the Anishnabeg, the Chippewa, the Haudenosaunee, and the Wendat peoples, and is now home to many diverse First Nations, Inuit, and Métis peoples. We acknowledge that Toronto is covered by Treaty 13 with the Mississaugas of the Credit. We are grateful to live and work on this land.

Cover design by Ingrid Paulson; cover art John James Audubon, *Farm-yard Fowls*, c. 1827, courtesy National Gallery of Art, Washington
Interior design by Crystal Sikma
Author photo by Andrés Simón Márquez

Coach House Books
80 bpNichol Lane
Toronto ON M5S 3J4
Canada

mail@chbooks.com
www.chbooks.com